by Michael Kogge

Based on the screenplay by
Lawrence Kasdan & J. J. Abrams
and
Michael Arndt

EGMONT
We bring stories to life

EGMONT

We bring stories to life

First published in Great Britain 2016
by Egmont UK Limited, The Yellow Building,
1 Nicholas Road, London W11 4AN

© & ™ 2016 Lucasfilm Ltd.

ISBN 978 1 4052 8393 9
64501/1

Printed in UK

To find more great *Star Wars* books, visit
www.egmont.co.uk/starwars

A long time ago in a galaxy far,
far away....

Luke Skywalker has vanished.
In his absence, the sinister
FIRST ORDER has risen from
the ashes of the Empire
and will not rest until
Skywalker, the last Jedi,
has been destroyed.

With the support of the
REPUBLIC, General Leia Organa
leads a brave RESISTANCE.
She is desperate to find her
brother Luke and gain his
help in restoring peace and
justice to the galaxy.

Leia has sent her most daring
pilot on a secret mission
to Jakku, where an old ally
has discovered a clue to
Luke's whereabouts....

PROLOGUE

ONCE there was an Old Republic, a just and benevolent government that united the galaxy for a thousand years. Under its grand democracy, peace reigned supreme. Science and technology expanded. New star systems were discovered and settled. The arts flourished. Citizens openly spoke their minds. A Galactic Senate was established, giving each member world a voice in the government. But as with anything that grows old, the Republic began to decline. Parts decayed. Its core turned rotten. War became a daily tragedy. When the Republic was finally pronounced dead, it was already a faded memory in the minds of its former citizens.

Once there was a mystical order of Jedi Knights, the guardians of peace and justice in the Old Republic. Legends told that they possessed abilities beyond the ordinary, including powers of the mind, of invisible strength, of foresight and wisdom. But as wise as they were, the Jedi were not wise enough to see the evil within their beloved Republic. Those whom the

Jedi had trusted as friends and allies betrayed and murdered them.

Once there was a Galactic Empire, born from the ashes of the Republic, yet the opposite of everything for which the Republic had ever stood. This was no grand democracy; a tyrannical Emperor ruled with an iron fist. Liberties were abolished. Obedience was mandated. Propaganda infected the arts. Science and technology expanded only for the benefit of the military. Star systems new and old were conquered and plundered. Citizens lived in fear of punishment if they spoke out against Imperial abuse. The Senate was disbanded. The Jedi were exterminated. The only voice that mattered was that of the Emperor. But try as he might, he could not extinguish all the flames of hope.

Once there was a Rebellion, sparked by a passionate few who cherished the principles of the Republic and despised the Empire. At first it was a ragtag alliance of defiant freethinkers, maverick artists, enlightened nobles and restless youths. It began its fight against the Empire unorganised. Small and weak. Unable to win a skirmish, let alone a war. Though the losses piled up and victory seemed impossible, these rebels did not surrender. They found hope in the heroics of a young man named Luke Skywalker. By learning the way of the Jedi, he helped bring an end to the tyranny. So as quickly as the Empire rose, it fell. A New Republic was founded in its wake.

Once a war starts, however, it is almost impossible to stop. Such was the case when the New Republic struggled to keep the peace. For not all were swayed back to democracy. Civil war had hardened many hearts. Worlds that championed Imperial discipline broke away from the New Republic and renamed themselves the First Order. Their goal was to destroy the New Republic and return the galaxy to the false glories of the Empire. But few in the New Republic saw the First Order as a serious threat. Those who did mounted a counteroffensive; yet against the rising military might of the First Order, the Resistance seemed too little, too late.

And the one who might have the power to aid their cause, a man by the name of Luke Skywalker, was nowhere to be found.

CHAPTER
1

WAR was coming to the planet Jakku.

Its herald was the colossal battle cruiser known as the *Finalizer*. It soared through the depths of space with little worry of ambush. Nearly three kilometres from bow to stern, the Star Destroyer bristled with turbolaser cannons, tractor beams, shield generators and missile launchers. And that was only its exterior.

The interior of the *Finalizer* housed its true firepower – its crew. Thousands of officers, gunners, soldiers and technicians were unified in one purpose: make the First Order the dominant power in the galaxy. Their devotion to the cause was unshakable, and that loyalty bred a deadly efficiency. Orders were carried out, exactly as instructed, without thought of moral consequence. For in the minds of the crew, the First Order was always right.

The soldiers who executed the will of the First Order in combat were called stormtroopers. And like the First

Order's Star Destroyers, sight of them inspired not only dread but awe.

The stormtroopers wore the white body armour that had been perhaps the most recognisable symbol of the former Empire, but that armour had been refined. The shell plates were lightened and made less bulky, which provided greater flexibility and freedom of movement. And that singular face of Imperial brutality - the stormtrooper helmet - was streamlined. Its visor was elongated to permit a larger field of vision while still keeping its vague resemblance to a human skull.

But these First Order troopers were more than just ordinary soldiers in terrifying costumes. It was their skill in combat that set them apart. They had been selected to join the ranks in childhood. The stormtrooper corps had become their family. Their alphanumeric call signs had become their names. Their training was so thorough, so disciplined that nothing frightened them. They would sacrifice their lives without hesitation. They would commit the unspeakable if commanded. Guilt never troubled them. The First Order was always right.

Having recently been commissioned as a full stormtrooper, FN-2187 was eager to do his duty.

FN-2187 advanced with his squad into a desert settlement. Most of the villagers had fled, though a few, dressed in not much more than rags, mounted a defense. It proved feeble and short-lived. For every shot from a villager's sporting blaster or slugthrower, the stormtroopers fired many times with their rifles. The first trooper to return fire was almost always FN-2187. His latest shot had downed a rooftop sniper.

'Can you give others a chance, Eight-Seven? Had that last target in my sights,' said FN-2003 over the helmets' internal comms.

'Why? So you can miss, Slip?' replied FN-2199, who went by the nickname Nines.

'Slip can miss all he wants, but I need a kill,' said FN-2000, or Zeroes, as everyone in the training cadre knew him. 'Not fair that Eight-Seven gets all the glory.'

According to a counter displayed inside FN-2187's helmet readout, he had eliminated more targets than any other trooper in the squad. The distinction didn't make him proud; he was just doing his job.

FN-2187's infrared sensors picked up a flicker of movement across the street. He magnified the view. A woman with dirt-caked hair crouched behind an animal hitching post. Trembling, her teeth chattering, she stared at the troopers and reached into her pocket. What she pulled out was dark and round, the same shape as a grenade.

'Down, everyone!' FN-2187 dropped to the ground. His comrades did the same.

A heartbeat from pulling his trigger, FN-2187's helmet recognised the object in the woman's hand as a native *gugu* fruit. She bit into it, probably to still her clacking teeth and calm her fright.

The comm chatter became laughter. 'Beware edible missiles,' Nines joked. 'Can stain your armour.'

Zeroes rose and adjusted his chest plate. 'Mine's dented now. Thanks, Eight-Seven.'

'I do what I can,' FN-2187 said, taking their ribbing in stride. He'd almost shot someone who wasn't an enemy combatant. He needed to be more careful.

A black-gloved hand reached down to help him up. It was FN-2003. Slip. 'No matter what we say, Eight-Seven, yours was incredible reaction time for target reassessment.'

'Doubt I would've been able to desist from pulling my trigger,' added Nines.

'That's why you're always running out of ammo, Nines,' Zeroes said. All four squad mates laughed.

The incessant sound of warfare stopped. 'Troopers, stand down,' came a stern voice over hidden loudspeakers. 'Simulation is complete.'

The desert village disappeared and FN-2187 and the other troopers of the squad found themselves standing in the white void of the *Finalizer's* simulation room. The thousands of pinholes that pricked the walls, ceiling, and floor no longer projected the holographic images that had made their training exercise seem so real.

'Assemble for imminent deployment,' the bodiless voice boomed.

Heading with his squad towards the hangar, FN-2187 noticed a palpable excitement among his comrades. FN-2187 felt it himself, along with a sense of relief. There would be no more simulations. They were about to embark on their first true combat mission.

In the docking bay, three other stormtrooper squads joined them from opposite entrances. They all marched past racks of TIE fighters and came to a halt at precisely the same time, equidistant from Captain Phasma, leader of the First Order's stormtrooper legions.

Phasma stood before four troop transports. Her spotless chrome armour gleamed. The mantle of her command, a black cape with red-striped edge, hung across her body from a clasp on her left shoulder.

'Troopers,' she said, her voice modulated through her helmet, 'your objective is simple. Apprehend this fugitive of justice at all costs.' She held out a personal holopad. A miniature image of an old human male in sackcloth robes materialised above her palm. 'He goes by the name of Lor San Tekka and is a sworn enemy of the First Order. Request backup immediately if you find him. We want him brought in to First Order custody alive for interrogation.'

FN-2187 studied the bluish hologram of the man. The fugitive must be very important to warrant the First

Order's sending a Star Destroyer and four squads of stormtroopers to catch him.

'Are there any questions?' Phasma asked.

All troopers remained silent and motionless, rifles held in double-handed grips. Phasma took a step forward. 'For most of you, this will be your first experience of real combat. I cannot believe none of you have questions or concerns.'

FN-2187 lifted a hand.

'Speak, Two-One-Eight-Seven,' Phasma said.

FN-2187 returned his hand to his rifle. 'What about collateral damage? How do we prevent civilian casualties?'

'You don't,' Phasma said. 'These villagers may appear poor and defenseless, but by sheltering a known enemy, they have declared war on the First Order. If they do not surrender at once, do what is necessary.' She turned to address all the troopers. 'Is that understood?'

'Yes, Captain,' FN-2187 said, his voice drowned out in the chorus of his comrades.

'Everyone, remember not to overthink the situation. Trust your training, follow your orders, and you will all return victorious in no time.'

Phasma gestured with her rifle. 'You may board your assigned transport,' she said. 'Long live the First Order.'

FN-2187 and the stormtrooper chorus repeated the cry. 'Long live the First Order!'

The troopers saluted Captain Phasma as they marched past her into the transports. Her gaze seemed to linger on FN-2187 for a moment longer than the others. Or maybe that was just his nerves. He knew Phasma expected great things from him. In the past, she had praised him before his peers as one of the strongest of the new cadets. But he wasn't a cadet anymore. He was a stormtrooper of the First Order, about to test his mettle in the 'real thing,' a life-or-death scenario. On this mission, he could show his comrades that he deserved to be in their ranks. He could prove to Captain Phasma and the First Order that he was worth their investment in him.

In step with his squad, FN-2187 saluted his captain and boarded the transport, ready to take on the Resistance.

One benefit of being a starfighter pilot was that you got to travel the galaxy. Flying for the New Republic and then the Resistance, Poe Dameron had seen it from Rim to Core. Lifeless hunks of rock. Forest moons. Mud planets that nearly swallowed his X-wing. And more than his fair share of desert worlds, like Jakku.

General Leia Organa had sent him here on a secret mission, 'a mission vital to the survival of the Resistance,' she had told him. A mission that might help her find her long-lost brother, Luke Skywalker.

So far, the mission had gone by the book. He had slipped into Jakku's atmosphere under cover of darkness and concealed his X-wing under a dense outcropping of rock. He'd instructed his spherical astromech droid, BB-8, to do reconnaissance while he put on his flight jacket and journeyed through the cold desert night to the nearby village of Tuanul. Here, among the tents and hovels, lived Lor San Tekka, the man Poe was tasked to contact.

The villagers weren't an overly friendly bunch, but they also didn't bother him. Jakku was a world where everyone minded their own business, for good reason. The galaxy was a big place, teeming with worlds harbouring more temperate climates. Those who eked out an existence on the desert planet were either born here or trying to hide. Best not to ask questions or cast odd glances; you could never be sure whom you might annoy.

Tekka did not seem surprised in the least by Poe's arrival. He gestured Poe inside his hut and greeted the pilot with a warm smile. Tekka was human and old – very old – wrinkled by more than a few lifetimes' worth of worry lines. The man would have been in his prime during the Clone Wars, a conflict that had raged more than half a century before. The galaxy had undergone so much change since then, and a man as advanced in years as Tekka had witnessed it all.

The old man stood tall and strong, showing none of the usual infirmities of the elderly. When he spoke to Poe, his tones were warm and genuine, as if they'd been acquaintances their entire lives. They made small talk, which was part of the game, so as to sound inconspicuous to any listeners. But the small talk ended when Tekka gave Poe a slim leather bag, then placed his own hand on top of it. 'This will make things right.' He removed his hand, leaving Poe holding the bag.

'Legend says this map was unobtainable,' Poe said. 'How'd you do it?'

The old man just smiled at him, and Poe smiled back. 'You're not gonna tell me a thing, are you? That's all right.' He gripped the bag tightly. 'I've heard stories about your adventures since I was a kid. It's an honour to meet you.'

The old man acknowledged Poe's admiration with a grave face. 'I've travelled too far to ignore the collective anguish that threatens to drown the galaxy in a flood of dark despair,' he said. 'Something must be done – whatever the cost, whatever the danger. Without the Jedi, there can be no balance in the Force, and all will be given over to the dark side.'

Poe knew better than to converse about the Jedi or the Force. Such topics were above his pay grade. 'The general's been after this a long time,' he said.

'"General."' The old man's smile returned. 'To me, she's royalty.'

'Yeah, but don't call her "Princess,"' Poe advised. 'Not to her face. She really doesn't like it.'

He was about to depart when BB-8 spun into the hut. Those ignorant of the droid's capabilities often commented on how adorable he looked. Some likened his domed head and round body to an overturned fruit bowl atop an orange-and-white gravball. But looks could deceive, for it was this design that made BB-8 a most adept companion in matters of espionage. The droid reported what he had seen in his reconnaissance outside the village to Poe in urgent beeps.

Poe took out his quadnoculars and hurried outside, with Tekka behind him.

Focused on the sky, the quadnocs revealed four transports dropping fast. Poe recognised the make and model of the transports instantly. First Order.

War was coming to the planet Jakku.

CHAPTER
2

A SPIRIT of camaraderie pervaded the First Order transport. Backs were slapped. Weapons inspected. Light-hearted taunts exchanged. Would FN-2000 transmit accurate location data? Would FN-2199 run out of blaster packs? Would FN-2003 be able to keep up, or would he slip behind the rest? Would FN-2187 keep his helmet on?

FN-2187 laughed with his comrades, but he knew he should be focused and not let his exuberance for the mission cloud his preparation. FN-2003's supportive nod reassured FN-2187 that the excitement was mutual. The troop transport shuddered when it hit the ground. FN-2187 stood firm. Unshakable. Immovable. At the ready. His squad mates did the same. It was their moment. It was what they had trained for years to do. They would look back on this day as the beginning of what would be a long and storied career in the stormtrooper corps.

The hatch lifted. The ramp extended. FN-2187's

helmet visor compensated for the dark of night. He would be able to see potential enemies in the infrared. But it took longer for the dust from the landing to settle and permit FN-2187 a full view of the battlefield.

The village was smaller and sadder than what had been portrayed in the simulations. Its tattered tents and sand-blasted hovels hardly seemed a proper sanctuary for Resistance fighters. But FN-2187's duty wasn't to question his superiors. It was to follow them. The First Order was always right.

FN-2003 nudged his shoulder. FN-2187 nudged back.

The signal was given.

FN-2187 marched out with his comrades into battle.

Poe climbed into his X-wing cockpit and switched on its systems. He felt guilty making an escape when First Order stormtroopers were attacking Tuanul. But Lor San Tekka would not let him stay. He said that Poe's mission was too important. The stakes too high. The fate of the entire galaxy depended on Poe's delivering the artifact he'd received from Lor San Tekka.

The *entire galaxy.* Tekka sure didn't mince words.

BB-8 rocked back and forth in the astromech socket behind the cockpit. The droid was getting impatient. 'We're going, we're going,' Poe said.

He activated the repulsors and began to edge the

craft out from under the stone outcropping. Within moments, he'd have a clear path to launch.

There was a high-pitched *ping-ping* and the ship suddenly shook. Poe snatched the flight stick to prevent the X-wing from careening into the surrounding rock. They were taking enemy fire. The scanner showed two stormtroopers rushing at the craft, rifles raised.

The troopers weren't on their feet long. Poe triggered his fighter's drop-down laser cannon, setting the troopers ablaze, along with much of the neighbouring vegetation.

More troopers would be on the way. Poe had to leave. He dismissed all prechecks and started the engines. The X-wing rattled in response.

Poe sprang out of the cockpit and scrambled down the fuselage. BB-8 popped out of the socket to roll with him.

The damage was worse than Poe had feared. Two of the engines smoked, struck at the weak points. Those First Order troopers had known the precise locations that would knock out an X-wing. Poe would not be leaving Jakku anytime soon.

He retrieved the leather bag Tekka had given him and removed what it held: a curious object resembling a bundle of silver blocks of varying sizes. The blocks were all adhered to one another, and some had red squares and rectangles visible along the sides. The item was so small yet so crucial to preserving all that was good in the galaxy.

Size never determined significance. BB-8 proved that every day. That's why Poe trusted the little droid to keep safe what Tekka had given him and complete the mission in his absence.

He inserted the object into BB-8's frontal data slot. 'Get as far away from here as you can. I'll come back for you.'

The droid shrilled a negative, not wanting to leave his master.

'Go!' Poe said, then lowered his voice. He regarded his loyal companion with an affection few humans extended to mechanicals. 'I'm gonna take out as many of those bucketheads as I can. It'll be all right. I'll come back for you.'

BB-8 beeped rebuttals, but Poe would not be swayed. 'Go on! It'll be all right,' he repeated.

The little droid wheeled away, holding in his memory banks information vital to the security of the Resistance - a clue to the whereabouts of Luke Skywalker, last of the Jedi.

CHAPTER
3

THE battle to take Tuanul proved to be nothing like the simulations FN-2187 and his squad had practised. The villagers did not shrink in terror or surrender to the gleaming stormtroopers. Instead, they fought back with a ferocity never exhibited by training drones or holographic soldiers. Some rushed the troopers head-on, firing their hunting weapons. Others hid behind crates and picked off troopers at random. You could die and never know you were shot.

As part of the last squad to arrive on the scene, FN-2187 hadn't even triggered his sidearm when FN-2003 crumpled to the ground, his armour smoking. FN-2187 dropped down beside his buddy immediately. He wanted to render some kind of medical aid, but the wound was too severe. The trooper they all called Slip was beyond help.

FN-2187 stared at FN-2003. Only Slip's fingers were exposed, reaching out of a ripped and bloody glove.

The inside of FN-2187's helmet became wet, and not from sweat. He was relieved Slip could not see his face. His tears would have betrayed their countless hours of training and discipline.

FN-2003's fingers stopped reaching.

After paying his friend a moment of respect, FN-2187 rose. He staggered forward into the village, unthinking. Fires ignited by flametroopers consumed buildings and bodies. Smoke covered it all like a shroud.

Rounding a corner, he came upon a villager who wasn't a corpse. Instinctively, he lifted his blaster. She halted. She had no helmet to hide her fear. Fear that this was the end, that FN-2187 would fire his rifle and consign her body to the flames.

FN-2187 lowered his weapon. The woman didn't move. She stared at him, confused. He looked at her and thought of Slip.

A sonic boom ended that fixation. She fled. FN-2187 craned his head.

A sleek shuttlecraft folded its wings and descended to land. It was of a class reserved only for the highest members of the First Order.

Once firmly on the ground, the shuttle's hatch opened. Out stepped a man cowled in a dark cloak. Over his face he wore a banded metal mask.

He was one of the Supreme Leader's top enforcers, Kylo Ren.

FN-2187 couldn't take his eyes off of Ren, who walked towards the heart of the fight that was still raging. Every step conveyed strength and power.

A hard tap from behind caused FN-2187 to stumble. One of the squadron commanders stood over him. 'Back to your team. This isn't over yet.'

FN-2187 did as told, though not without a glance back. The striking figure of Kylo Ren was gone, however, lost in the black smoke of the battle.

When BB-8 was safely away, Poe Dameron headed towards the village, hoping he might be able to save some of the innocent residents from being slaughtered.

Smoke and debris concealed him from stormtroopers but not from the open eyes of the corpses he stepped over. Their deaths reminded him why he had joined the Resistance. The First Order resorted to only one strategy in resolving conflicts: violence.

Two figures conversed ahead. Poe approached with caution. One was none other than Lor San Tekka, standing tall in his desert robes. But the other figure nearly made Poe run back to his X-wing.

Poe had been warned about this man. His name was Kylo Ren, and he looked as if he'd stepped from the darkest pages of galactic history. He was dressed all in black. A wide belt circled his waist and a dark cloak hung from his shoulders. He wore a hood over his head. His face was veiled by a metal mask.

Maintaining his cover, Poe strained to listen to the two men. It proved difficult at that distance, with explosions from the continuing battle, but he thought he heard Tekka say that Ren did not belong with the First Order. That Ren had turned away from his own heritage.

What was clear was that Ren wanted something from the old man, and Tekka wouldn't give it to him.

Poe drew his blaster and left his cover. He needed to get closer to have the best shot at killing Ren. If he missed, he doubted Ren would give him a second chance.

Poe heard their conversation as he advanced towards them. 'You may try,' Tekka told Ren, 'but you cannot deny the truth that is your family.'

Ren appeared to rise in stature. A metallic cylinder flew into his hand. From it ignited a fiery crimson blade. Two quarter beams formed a hilt. It was the legendary weapon of the Jedi Knights. A lightsaber.

'So true,' Ren snarled through his mask.

He swung his saber through the defenseless old man. Lor San Tekka never spoke again.

Poe Dameron cried out, firing at Ren. He didn't let his finger off the trigger. It didn't matter. Ren whirled, holding up an open palm. Poe's shots fizzled in thin air, one frozen in flight, crackling with energy.

Poe was correct that he wouldn't get a second

chance to kill Ren. He might not get a second chance to do anything. One look from Ren and Poe froze. He was suddenly unable to fire his blaster, or even move his limbs. The masked man's diabolical gaze seemed to hold Poe in a state of paralysis.

Two stormtroopers yanked Poe towards Ren. Poe couldn't struggle in their grip, because he couldn't move. Kylo Ren retracted his lightsaber blade and clipped its hilt to his belt. He peered at Poe, his eyes hidden behind the visor of his mask.

Poe tried to appear unconcerned about his present situation. 'Who talks first? Do you talk first? Do I talk first?'

'A Resistance pilot, by the look of him,' Ren said to the troopers, ignoring Poe's questions. 'Search him.'

One trooper performed Ren's request with thuggish delight, smacking rather than patting Poe down. The other swept a personal scanner across Poe's body from head to toe.

Disappointed in his examination, the trooper who'd roughly handled Poe reported to Ren. 'Nothing, sir.'

The second trooper looked up from his scanner readout. 'Same here, sir. Internally, this one is clean. Terminate him?'

Poe did not wither under the masked man's gaze. If Poe was going to die here, he would do so in defiance.

'No,' Ren said. 'Keep him.'

The troopers dragged Poe away. Once out of Ren's presence, Poe could finally move his muscles.

Sadly, he was in no shape to use those muscles to respond to the screams he heard coming from the village. Kylo Ren may have spared Poe's life, for the moment, but those remaining villagers met a different fate. A round of blaster fire hushed their cries for good.

As he was thrown into a troop transport, Poe wondered whether joining the villagers might have been more desirable than where he was heading.

At least BB-8 was still out there, somewhere.

CHAPTER
4

ON JAKKU, whenever there was a mention of Star Destroyers, glances weren't directed to the skies but to the distant sands. For if one travelled deep into the desert past Niima Outpost, that's precisely what one would find. Jutting out from the dunes like enormous, half-buried arrowheads loomed the mountainous wreckage of Imperial Star Destroyers. Scraps of smaller starships lay littered around the crashed titans, all relics of a terrible battle that best remained forgotten.

Most avoided that graveyard at all costs. Jakku's pounding windstorms had eroded the derelicts into veritable death traps. Rusty floors could crumble under the feet of unfortunate visitors. Beams could teeter and collapse. Old pipes could burst, spraying hazardous fluids.

Rey was not afraid. She didn't have that luxury. If she couldn't brave such dangers, she couldn't afford to eat.

She hung on to the wall of a demolished destroyer and used her tools to wiggle free various components that rust hadn't devoured. The ship was a treasure trove of metal sheeting and military-grade tech that, if given a proper cleaning, could fetch Rey a meal or two at Niima Outpost.

She was nineteen and this was her life. Her days were spent venturing into perilous places and collecting what others called trash. Admittedly, she had a knack for scavenging, but she didn't do it by choice. Legitimate jobs on Jakku were as scarce as water. She had to make do with what was available – which meant salvaging scrap from junkyards and trading it to Unkar Plutt for ration packets of food.

Having gathered as much as she could, Rey climbed down the wall slowly and carefully. Outfitted in tan desert garb, with green goggles shielding her eyes, an overstuffed backpack on her shoulders, and her staff wedged through the straps, she felt akin to the steelpeckers that also scavenged these parts. They swarmed the premises at night, chewing on corroded metal and loose wiring, helping turn the destroyers into dust.

Rey dropped to the ground near a chunk of salvage she'd previously found. She lifted it with both arms, her muscles aching under its weight. But her stomach would ache more if she didn't take it with her.

Jakku's blazing sun welcomed her when she emerged from the interior of the destroyer. She set down her salvage, pushed her goggles away from her eyes, and drank from her canteen.

Standing on that perch, she had a full view of the junkyard around her. Sand had shrouded most of the smaller craft from the battle of years past. But here and there, something metallic poked out, such as the solar panel of a TIE fighter or the nose of an old X-wing.

Holding the canteen over her mouth, she tapped its side, desperate for every last drop. When nothing more came, she clipped it to her belt. She hoped that what she'd salvaged here would be able to quench her thirst and feed her belly for the night.

Rey deposited her salvage onto a sled of scrap metal, then shoved it down a slope. Her speeder was parked below. It wasn't anything to look at, not much more than a box with engines. But her present line of work didn't require anything else.

Finding a larger sheet of scrap, Rey positioned herself on it and went sledding down the dune after her salvage. Skidding to a halt at the bottom, she jettisoned the sled, loaded her speeder with her loot, and soon was racing off to Niima Outpost. Breakfast, lunch and dinner awaited – she hoped.

Arriving at Niima Outpost, Rey parked her speeder and took her salvage into an open-air structure canopied from the sun. The place served primarily as a cleaning station for those who dealt with the junk dealer, Unkar Plutt. At long workbenches, individuals of many species brushed and buffed their day's booty. The newer and shinier the scrap looked, the more portions of food Plutt would pay out. Rey found an open space and started scrubbing.

After she'd done the best she could to make her junk look like expensive junk, Rey went to Plutt. This was her least favourite part of the day. The blubbery Crolute cooled himself in a shed built from cargo crawler panelling, where he judged the values of both salvage and scavenger like a tin-pot prince. He definitely looked the part: a leather cap crowned his fat, bald head, and piles of flesh drooped around his neck like a royal mantle. His body was as bloated as his sense of his own generosity. He loved pretending to be charitable in his appraisals, when in truth there was no greedier individual on Jakku.

Rey waited before Plutt's booth while he inspected her prizes in his fleshy hands. 'A decent offering, if nothing remarkable,' Plutt said, fingering her salvage. 'Today you get a quarter portion.'

A quarter portion, for usable metal and Star Destroyer components? Rey wanted to scream. Plutt was ripping her off. On any other planet, what she had given him would've netted her enough to live on for a month, at least.

Unfortunately, Jakku wasn't any other planet. It was an isolated world where the bare necessities were worth more than rare metals and military tech. To make matters worse, Plutt had bought out or beaten up all his competition at Niima Outpost, giving him a monopoly over the local junk exchange. If Rey wanted to be fed, even in quarter portions, she had to go through him.

From the booth's transfer drawer, she accepted the two ration packets. One contained a brown flour substance, the other a green protein square.

'That's my girl,' Plutt said.

She hated being called that.

Rey made dinner in her humble home. She opened both ration packets and dumped the green protein square into a pan on a burner. While that was cooking, she mixed the brownish flour with water in a container. The chemical reaction worked its magic and a doughy loaf rose.

'Meat and bread' was what Plutt called this packet combination, though Rey doubted it tasted anything like the real thing. She ate from a plate that she licked clean of any leftover food. Through a blast hole that now was a window, she saw the lines of smoke from a ship departing over Niima Outpost. She wiped her mouth on her sleeve and took stock of her few possessions. They always brightened her day and reminded her that there was more to the galaxy than life on Jakku.

She had a doll she'd sewn together as a younger girl from the fabric of an orange flight suit. A canister stored rare flowers she'd plucked in the desert. Then there was the computer Rey had built out of scavenged parts. She had loaded it with a flight simulator program to practise her starship piloting. Rey's sleeping area contained her single luxury, a bloggin-feather pillow. Last, a banged-up pilot's helmet she'd found in a Rebellion-era X-wing rested on a shelf. This was something she couldn't toss away or redeem as salvage. It would be like dishonouring the pilot who had worn it.

She took the helmet off its shelf and put it over her head, then went out to look at the setting sun. The helmet's polarised visor protected her eyes and allowed Rey to watch the sun sink towards the horizon. She owed her survival to those who had donned helmets like this. The great battle they'd waged supplied her with scraps to sell and had given her a place to live.

Humble, her home wasn't – not from the outside. Its rusted hulk spread across the surrounding salt flats like a giant fallen beast. She dwelled in its belly, an armoured midsection that once had carried squads of Imperial stormtroopers. A cockpit protruded like a head via a tubular neck. Four massive mechanical legs splayed out over the sand, frozen in a dead pose.

During the battle, this monstrosity of metal had plodded through the desert, scattering sand dunes and squashing soldiers. It must have terrified those who fell into its path of destruction. The Empire had classified it as an AT-AT – an All-Terrain Armoured Transport. Rey was more fond of its common name – 'walker' – or as she called it, 'home.'

A wail interrupted her thoughts. Strangely, it sounded nothing like the creatures that inhabited this part of the desert. It was high-pitched, almost . . . *electronic*?

She grabbed her staff from the walker, then ran out into the desert, heading towards the sound. It repeated, the same tone at a precise rate. Binary, from the sound of it. The language of droids.

Rey climbed to the top of a dune and saw that the cries came from a spherical droid with an astromech's dome. It rolled around in a net, getting itself more and more tangled. A Teedo tried to pull the trapped droid up onto the armoured luggabeast he rode.

Rey didn't begrudge scavengers, since she was one herself. But the small droid was putting up such a spirited defense that its capture seemed unjust. This unit wasn't the average binary loadlifter or probot spy. Its yelps were frantic pleas for aid, and Rey had a feeling the droid would try to assist her if their positions were reversed and *she* were caught in the net.

To grab the Teedo's attention, Rey shouted in his native language. Both captor and captive paused in their struggle and looked up at her. She continued shouting, ordering the Teedo to leave the droid alone. The reptilian Teedo hissed through his rusted mask.

Rey had experience interacting with this species. If she hinted that she was intimidated in the slightest, she would lose the contest of wills. So she drew her knife and went down the dune, staking her staff at the bottom.

The Teedo cursed her when she started to cut the droid out of the net, but he remained on his luggabeast and did not back up his words with action.

Still, Rey was not just going to allow herself to be insulted. She spewed out some harsh threats of her own, which she punctuated by brandishing her knife.

The Teedo replied with a foul-mouthed rant. But the end effect was that he reined his luggabeast around and lumbered away.

The droid rolled free of the net and piped angrily at its would-be captor. 'Shhh,' Rey said. She knelt on the droid's level. 'He's just a Teedo.'

Assessing the droid's condition, she noticed its antenna was bent. Scorch marks marred its dome. The little guy had seen some action. 'Where'd you come from?'

The droid blurted out something harsh. Rey scoffed. Her comfort with all things mechanical had made her fluent in binary. 'Classified? *Really?* Well, me too. Big secret. I'll keep mine and you can keep yours.'

She stood and pointed away from her home. 'Niima Outpost is that way. Stay off Kelvin Ridge. Keep away from the Sinking Fields up north or you'll drown in the sand. The closer you get to Niima, the less likely you are to run into a marauding Teedo.'

Her advice was not heeded. Instead, the droid

followed her as she headed to her walker. She stopped. 'You can't come with me. I don't want anyone with me. You understand?'

The droid whimpered. But this time, she wouldn't be manipulated. She had saved it, and that should be enough. 'No – and don't ask me again. I'm not your friend.'

She strode forward. The droid continued to beep. Soft and sad. Rey sighed. She turned around. The image of an astromech unit rolling alone through the desert did strike her as preposterous. If the droid didn't fall into a sand pit, capture by other Teedo tribesmen seemed likely. Particularly at night, when they lurked in greater numbers.

'In the morning, you go,' she told the droid. She received a grateful beep. 'Fine, you're welcome.' The droid continued to beep excitedly. She chuckled. 'Yes, there's a lot of sand here.'

The astromech formally introduced himself by chirping out his designation.

'Beebee-Ate? OK. Hello, Beebee-Ate. My name is Rey.' The droid inquired if she had a family name. 'No, just Rey.'

The questions continued. This unit was a chatterball. 'You're not going to talk all night, are you?'

BB-8 apologised with one last beep.

'Good,' Rey said.

They went into the walker, where they spent the night in peace and quiet. Somewhat.

CHAPTER
5

THE stormtroopers who had survived the raid disembarked from the troop transports into the docking bay of the *Finalizer*. A pair shoved the captured Resistance pilot towards the detention area. The rest rushed to the ready rooms to relieve themselves of their filthy armour.

FN-2187 would not be joining them.

He peeled away from his squad and leaned over the nearest waste container. Yanking off his blood-stained helmet, he let out everything in his stomach.

No matter how much he retched, he didn't feel any different. His sickness wasn't caused by anything he'd eaten. It was caused by what he'd seen and heard. What he'd participated in. What he'd failed to stop.

The atrocity that had occurred at Tuanul was burned into his memory like a blaster scar. The villagers had screamed and begged for their lives as they were lined up before the stormtrooper squad. The woman he'd let go stood among them. And there was nothing he could do to let her off the hook this time.

The order to execute the villagers came from the masked man in the black cloak, Kylo Ren, who relayed it to Captain Phasma. Waiting for her signal, FN-2187 and his squadmates lifted their blaster rifles.

'Fire!' Captain Phasma had said.

It was the first order FN-2187 had ever disobeyed. His comrades let loose a salvo that didn't require FN-2187's participation to be effective. He watched aghast as each and every one of those villagers crumpled and fell. The horrific sight triggered something deep inside of him. Anger. Guilt. A will of his own. It had churned up the sickness he now vomited into the waste container.

After many heaves, FN-2187 took a breath. He could tell no one how he felt. If his superiors found out, he would be interrogated, demoted, and perhaps even executed for rebellious thoughts. He'd have to keep his true feelings a secret.

He stood tall, in stormtrooper posture once again, and turned. He was surprised to find another trooper in brilliant chrome armour and a black officer's cape stood behind him.

'Eff-Enn-Two-One-Eight-Seven,' said Captain Phasma, 'I understand you experienced some difficulty with your weapon. Please be so good as to submit it for inspection.'

He glanced at the rifle he still carried. When asked

by a squad commander why he hadn't fired at the villagers, he had said his rifle jammed. But that was not an explanation Phasma would care to hear. His training had taught him there was only one proper response. 'Yes, Captain.'

She continued to look at him. 'And who gave you permission to remove that helmet?'

'Sorry, Captain.' He put his helmet back on.

'Report to my division at once,' she said.

Saluting, FN-2187 realised that keeping his secret from his superiors was not going to be easy. They would discover his treason. And they would view him no differently than the villagers. Expendable.

FN-2187 began to consider other options.

Stay here. I'll come back for you, sweetheart. I promise.

'Yes, I'm here, I'm here!' Rey shouted. Her eyes popped open and she looked about the walker. BB-8's dome lights glowed on low illumination. The doors were shut. Nothing in her home was out of place.

As always, there was no figure to the voice.

She'd been haunted by a dream. Or a nightmare. At this point in her life, she couldn't decide what it was. All she knew was the voice came and went as it pleased, sometimes staying absent for months. But when she least expected it, the voice would return, never leaving her alone permanently. Never.

She rose from her mat. The moment she did, BB-8 jumped to full illumination. Even at low power, BB-8's passive sensors were active.

Rey squinted in the light. 'Power back down, will you? You're hurting my eyes.'

BB-8's dome lights dimmed, though not without a worried query.

'I'm fine,' Rey said. 'I just need some air.'

She retrieved her staff and went outside. One could freeze in the desert at night. But Rey didn't go out to gaze at the stars. She went to sweat.

With her staff held in first position, Rey performed her exercise routine. Leaping, swinging, ducking, slashing. She pretended to fight invisible enemies, the numerous thugs of Jakku who were always trying to steal her salvage. She tossed her staff from hand to hand and twirled it in rapid fashion. She jabbed it into the sand and vaulted over it, never losing her grip.

If she was ever going to fall asleep that night and be rested for the next day's salvage, she'd have to exhaust herself.

Kylo Ren entered the detention cell. The prisoner, despite being bruised and battered, attempted to launch himself out of his chair. His bonds held, digging lines into his wrists and ankles.

Under his mask, Ren smiled. The suffering of his

enemies brought him pleasure. 'I had no idea we had the best pilot in the Resistance on board,' he said. The prisoner's name was Poe Dameron. Casualty reports from starfighter engagements indicated he had downed many brave First Order pilots.

'Revealing yourself through your futile attempt on my life was foolish. Even had you not been slow and ill-prepared, Tekka was already dead,' Ren said. Dameron struggled again in his chair. 'Comfortable?'

Dameron tried to move a hand. 'Not really.'

The pilot would regret his sarcasm after Ren was done with him. 'We both wanted the same thing from the old man. Perhaps he was more forthcoming with you than he was with me.'

'Might want to rethink your technique,' Dameron said.

Such a stupid man. He had no idea that the technique Ren was about to use would break him into a blabbering idiot. Soon Ren would know everything.

He reached towards the prisoner with gloved fingers. Through them Ren channelled currents of pain from his own bottomless well – and tendrils that would probe the depths of Dameron's weak mind.

'Tell me. Tell me.'

Dameron sat straight up, eyes bloodshot, in silent mental agony. As Ren expected, the pilot told.

Once in possession of the information, Kylo Ren

went to the destroyer's bridge, where he informed General Hux, the commander of the ship. 'The map to Skywalker's location is in a droid. An ordinary Beebee-Ate unit.'

The straw-haired general in the black uniform, whose brilliance had pushed him up the chain of command at a young age, glanced out the viewport at Jakku. 'That makes it easy, then. The directions are in a droid, and the droid is still on the planet.'

Ren followed General Hux's gaze out the viewport. He neglected to say that nothing was ever easy when it came to finding Luke Skywalker.

Rey finished her day's work a few hours earlier than usual, in large part due to BB-8. The diminutive droid couldn't carry anything, of course, but his sensors helped Rey locate the best salvage. While his constant beeping irritated her, it did make the hours seem to go by quicker. And though she'd never wanted a friend, the fact that she could vent her frustrations to someone who listened – even if that someone was a droid – took some of the edge off of living on Jakku.

But it was temporary. Soon everything would return to normal. She'd be alone again.

In payment for his assistance in the junkyards, Rey took BB-8 to Niima Outpost to find him transport off the planet.

'There's a trader in bay three who might be willing to give you a lift, wherever you're going,' she said. 'So, goodbye.'

Hoisting her satchel, she started towards Unkar Plutt's booth. BB-8 mewled like a happabore pup. Rey stopped and turned. 'Don't give up. He still might show, whoever your classified friend is,' she said with a wise look. 'Trust me. I know all about waiting.'

BB-8 murmured something long and full of concern. It astounded Rey that the droid could express such a wide spectrum of emotions only in beeps. She went back and knelt before BB-8.

'I'm waiting for my family.' Her eyes grew wet at the memory. 'They'll be back, one day.'

She had never admitted that to anyone. Rarely to herself. That a simple droid could pull the statement out of her stunned her.

BB-8 adjusted the magnification of his photoreceptor and beeped sympathetically.

'What? No – I'm not crying!' She blinked away the tears, rose and walked away from the prying machine. What was wrong with her? Crying in front of a droid?

BB-8 rolled alongside her, jabbering that his data showed otherwise. His sensors had registered condensation in her eyes.

'I wasn't crying!' But she was. Still. No matter how many times she blinked, the tears kept coming. So she gave up and let them fall and let the droid follow, answering none of his queries.

She decided against polishing her salvage that day. Best to get the exchange done with and go back home. There she could be alone, and sleep, and forget about everything.

When it was her turn, she went up and laid her satchel on the counter. Plutt appraised its contents. 'Two interlifts,' he said, scrutinising the two most valuable components she had salvaged that day. 'I'll give you one quarter portion. For the pair.'

The offer insulted her. She'd rather go hungry for the night than let him swindle her so blatantly. 'Last week they were a half portion each, and you said you are looking for more.'

'Conditions have changed.' The rings of fat around Plutt's neck wriggled as he looked past her. 'But what about the droid?'

The question surprised her. She glanced back. 'What about him?'

Plutt slobbered over himself. 'I'll pay for him.'

'How much?'

BB-8 started to emit worried beeps.

'Sixty portions,' Plutt said.

Did Rey hear him right? Did he say *sixty portions*? No way would Plutt ever offer such an amount, even for a functioning droid. Sixty portions would fill her stomach for weeks, even *months* if she was frugal. Surely Plutt had misspoken.

But the junk dealer eyed the droid and did not revise his offer. This made Rey suspicious. If there was one thing Rey knew about Unkar Plutt, it was that he was as honest as a Teedo marauder was polite. Plutt's appraisals were always well below market value. It was how he stayed rich and kept all the scavengers poor.

BB-8 bumped her leg, protesting frantically. Rey keyed a command on his dome. He instantly went mute, and his dome slid down to clunk against the ground.

Rey felt a pang of guilt, but at that price she'd be a loon not to sell the droid. Anyone in her boots would do the same. It was a matter of survival.

And she wasn't finished negotiating. For once, she had the upper hand. She had something Plutt truly wanted and she wasn't going to allow him to cheat her.

'One hundred portions,' she said.

Plutt's blubber rippled in contempt. 'One hundred it is,' he said.

The quickness of his acceptance alarmed her. She suddenly felt that she'd bargained too low and that Plutt had fleeced her once again.

She looked at BB-8, unmoving in the grit of the road. What was so valuable about that little droid?

CHAPTER
6

FN-2187 made a choice. Or more truthfully, after he'd considered all his options that didn't involve interrogation, imprisonment, or execution, the choice made him.

He couldn't have stopped the massacre on Jakku if he'd wanted. His squad mates would've turned their rifles on him. But there was something he might be able to do. Someone he might be able to save from Kylo Ren.

The junior officer manning the detention centre control station looked bleary-eyed from having to do multiple shifts while the raid on Jakku took place. He didn't object when FN-2187 entered and said he'd come to relieve him of his duty. Eager to be released, the young man forgot to hand over his security badge until FN-2187 asked.

Once the junior officer had left, FN-2187 went to the cell number that he'd overheard two troopers in the mess hall mention. He passed the badge over the sensor. The cell door swished open.

A single trooper stood guard in the cell. The dark-haired Resistance pilot, manacled to a chair, appeared to have taken both a physical and mental beating.

'I'm taking the prisoner to Kylo Ren,' FN-2187 told the cell guard.

Mere mention of Ren's name provoked the guard to action. He freed the prisoner from the chair and lifted him to his feet. FN-2187 did the rest, shoving the pilot through the doorway. He kept his blaster muzzle trained on the man's back and prodded him out of the detention centre. 'Turn here.'

When they were in a dark, vacant corridor, FN-2187 grabbed the pilot and steadied him. 'Listen carefully and pay attention. You do exactly as I say. I can get you out of here.'

The pilot gaped at him, still out of sorts. 'If . . . what – *who* . . . are you?'

FN-2187 took off his helmet. 'Would you be quiet and just listen to me? This is a rescue. I'm helping you escape. Can you fly a TIE fighter?'

Some life returned the pilot's eyes. 'What's going on here? Are you . . . are you with the Resistance?'

FN-2187 checked himself from impulsively reaffirming his allegiance to the First Order, which was how he'd been trained to answer such a question. 'No, I'm just breaking you out. Can you fly a—'

'I can fly anything,' the pilot said. 'But why are you helping me?'

FN-2187 peered down the corridor to scout for impending trouble. 'Because it's the right thing to do.'

The pilot eyed him skeptically. 'Buddy, if we're gonna do this, we have to be honest with each other.'

FN-2187 looked back at the pilot, exhaled, and told the truth. 'I need a pilot.'

The pilot grinned. 'Well, you just got me.'

'Yeah?'

'Yeah. We're gonna do this.'

FN-2187 nodded back, put on his helmet and pointed his gun at the man's back. The pilot resumed being a prisoner, lowering his head in submission as if heading to his doom.

They had no trouble until they arrived at the hangar. A few deck officers strolled past them, giving them sideways glances. 'Stay calm, stay calm,' FN-2187 murmured.

'I am calm,' the pilot muttered.

'I was talking to myself,' FN-2187 said.

'Oh, boy.'

FN-2187 didn't take offense at the pilot's sarcasm. First Order pilots exhibited similar arrogance. He took it as a sign that his prisoner was returning to normal.

He scanned the starfighters in the bay. Maintenance crew were working on most of the craft. But there was one that stood alone. Thick pylons mounted two hexagonal wings to the orb of its cockpit. Its chassis was painted black, with red marking one half of the cockpit and chrome glossing the wings' solar panels.

It would be the perfect getaway vessel. A Special Forces TIE fighter.

Once he saw the TIE fighter, Poe Dameron forgot about his pain.

Here was something he could handle. Two wings attached to twin ion engines. Built out of metal, held together by bolts. Nothing mystical about it, all mechanical.

They crossed the hangar deck, avoiding a maintenance droid, then climbed through the TIE's upper hatch into the command pod. Poe dropped into the pilot's chair while the trooper removed his helmet and took the gunner's seat on the other side, positioned back-to-back with Poe.

'I always wanted to fly one of these things.' Poe studied the controls. 'Can you shoot?'

'Anything designed for ground troops I can,' the trooper said. 'Like blasters.'

'The ship's guns work on the same principle. Only the results are a lot more expansive.' Poe pointed out the primary parts of the weapon systems. 'Let the autotargeting help you, and the triggers to fire.'

The trooper's hesitation didn't inspire confidence. 'This is . . . very complicated.'

Poe would have to wait to give a full tutorial. They needed to get out before the *Finalizer*'s crew discovered he was missing – if they hadn't already.

Poe activated the repulsors, but thick cables tethered the ship to the hangar deck.

Poe jostled the flight stick to try to pull free of the cables. Some snapped, but there were many more to go. Meanwhile, sirens began to blare throughout the hangar. The nearest stormtrooper patrol went into action. They rushed into the hangar, bringing heavy weapons to bear on the TIE.

'Now would be a good time to start shooting,' Poe said, ripping the ship free of more tethers.

The trooper experimented with the controls. 'I'll do my best. I'm not sure I can—'

Streaks of green erupted from the TIE's belly turret, laying waste to the hangar. Other TIEs tumbled off their racks to crash on the floor. The docking operations centre went to pieces. The attacking patrol didn't even fire their heavy weapons before a blast flattened them.

'Sorry, boys,' the trooper said.

Poe issued the command to switch off the magnetic shield that protected the open port from uninvited guests and unapproved departures. Since the TIE's lasers had obliterated the control room, the emergency circuits obeyed remote activation. Switching on the ion engines, Poe burned free of the last cables and the TIE rocketed out of the hangar.

He spun the fighter in barrel rolls, dodging turbolaser fire from the Star Destroyer. 'This thing really moves!'

Having gotten the gist of the guns, the trooper poured cannon fire back at the destroyer. His aimless shots were like those of a child playing his first hologame, sure to perplex the First Order crew inside the larger ship. The shots would have to start dismantling the turbolaser banks before enemy fire dismantled the TIE fighter.

'A target is coming to you – my left, your right,' Poe said. 'See it?'

'Hold on,' the trooper said. Poe heard him fumbling with the controls. 'I see it.'

A beep indicated the crosshairs had a lock, then the trooper triggered the guns. Less than a second later, the destroyer's turbolaser bank exploded.

The trooper whooped. 'You see that?'

'Told ya you could do it.' It struck Poe that the stormtrooper had saved his life twice, yet Poe didn't even know who the man was. 'What's your name?'

'Eff-Enn-Two-One-Eight-Seven.'

Poe glanced behind him. '"Eff-Enn" what?'

'That's the only name I was ever given,' said the trooper.

Hearing that rankled Poe. As a soldier himself, he

was offended that the First Order would attempt to erase the identities of the very individuals who were willing to die on the front lines. 'If that's the name they gave you, then I ain't using it,' he said. 'Eff-Enn, huh? I'm calling you Finn. That all right with you?'

The trooper hesitated. 'Yeah, "Finn,"' he said, trying out the name. He grinned. 'I like that.'

'I'm Poe. Poe Dameron.'

'Good to meet you, Poe.'

'Good to meet you, Finn.' Poe banked the TIE around for another attack run. Fleeing to jump to lightspeed was what the First Order would expect him to do. And that would be suicide. The time and distance necessary to manage a safe jump into hyperspace would supply plenty of free shots at the TIE.

Instead, Poe skimmed the fighter along the gigantic Star Destroyer's hull, presenting a more difficult target. The destroyer gunners risked hitting their own ship when shooting at the TIE. Finn also needed to be as close as he could to inflict maximum damage.

But after wreaking more havoc across the hull of the *Finalizer*, Poe didn't turn around for another go. He accelerated towards the only object in the vicinity that was larger than the Star Destroyer.

Finn turned in his seat to grab Poe's shoulder. 'Where are you going?'

'You mean, where are *we* going.' Poe pulled down

on the flight stick. A glowing tan orb appeared in the cockpit canopy. 'Back to Jakku, that's where.'

'What? *Jakku*? No, no, no,' Finn protested. 'For me and you, Jakku is another word for death. Poe, we gotta get out of this system!'

'And I have to get to my droid before the First Order does,' Poe said. Space around them bloomed with laser streaks as the *Finalizer* retrained its guns on them.

Finn sounded confused – too confused to return fire. 'Your . . . *droid*?'

Poe banked the TIE to starboard and port, eluding destruction by the slimmest margins. 'He's a BB unit. One of a kind. Orange and white.'

'I don't care what colour it is. No droid can be that important!'

'This one is, pal.' Poe pushed the engines for every last ion. 'My droid's got a map that leads to Luke Skywalker.'

The name hung in the air like a ghost. A ghost everyone in the First Order, from the lowest tech to the most decorated admiral, had been taught to loathe. They blamed the man with that name for the murders of their beloved Emperor and his most trusted envoy, Darth Vader.

'I never should have rescued you,' Finn said.

A tremendous blast of energy coincided with Finn's words. It buffeted the TIE, overwhelming the shields and killing an engine. The two passengers were shaken in their seats while their consoles sparked and smoked.

'All weapons systems are down – my controls are neutralised!' Finn said, coughing. 'You?'

Poe wanted to respond. He wanted to tell Finn to press the seat ejector. But his mouth wouldn't move. Neither would his hand. The pain he had forgotten about returned. Real pain. Physical pain. In his chest. Even his eyes. All he could see was the planet expanding before him, brighter and bigger until it blotted everything else out.

Perhaps Finn was right. Perhaps Jakku was death.

Poe blacked out.

One hundred portions. It was a number Rey couldn't refuse. It was a number that would change her life.

She stared at the little droid that would fetch such a tidy sum. BB-8's round body lay still, his dome resting in the dirt, like a deflated bounce ball discarded by some rich kid. Yet one person's trash was another's treasure. Unkar Plutt eyed the droid greedily – which caused Rey to again question the transaction.

'What are you going to do with the droid?'

Plutt stuffed the booth drawer with ration packets. 'Certain parties have been asking around for a droid like that.'

Certain parties? Who was Plutt talking about?

The drawer popped open on her side of the booth. At the sight of so much food, she reached down for a handful of packets.

'That's my girl,' Plutt said.

Those words made the rations look less than appetizing. Rey would lose something if she went through with the exchange, no matter how many portions Unkar gave her.

'Actually,' she said, taking none of the food packets, 'the droid's not for sale.'

The junk dealer's eyes bulged. His tone became less generous. 'Sweetheart, we already had a deal.'

'Conditions have changed,' Rey said, relishing his displeasure. The fat Crolute had changed his offers so many times in the past, turnabout was fair play.

She bent down to BB-8 and keyed the reactivation command. The droid's dome lit up and slid back atop his sphere.

'You have nothing,' Plutt bellowed at Rey. 'You *are* nothing!'

Rey didn't deny that as she walked away with BB-8, leaving the dealer to a tantrum in his stall. Yet the respectful looks from other scavengers made Rey certain of one thing.

She wasn't Plutt's girl.

CHAPTER
7

FINN. FN-2187. Finn. FN-2187.

He batted the two names around in his head as Jakku's winds batted him around in the ejection seat. What happened in the next few moments would seal his name and his fate. If his seat's booster rockets failed to fire or the parachute didn't release, he'd crash into the planetary surface and perish, remembered by those in the First Order as *renegade* trooper FN-2187.

But if he survived, his name would be whatever he chose to tell others.

The booster rockets fired. The black chute released. His descent slowed, almost imperceptibly at first but enough so that when he smashed into Jakku's surface, the impact only fractured his armour while his rattled bones stayed in his body.

He unbuckled himself and staggered to his feet. The desert of Jakku spread out as far as his eye could see.

Only to the east was the vista of sand broken. Smoke plumed into the sky.

He hastened towards it.

The crashed TIE fighter was still burning when he arrived. He stepped over sharp pieces of the fuselage to get closer. 'Poe? Say something if you can hear me – Poe!'

The elbow of an arm dangled out from what remained of the cockpit. He ran to it, grabbing and pulling. But the arm didn't belong to Poe. It belonged to Poe's empty flight jacket.

'Poe!'

The hot smoke obscured the inside of the cockpit, probably for the best. Flight jackets were manufactured with materials that could withstand high temperatures, but human skin still had its limits. Poe likely had been burnt beyond recognition.

The ground shifted, collapsing under the TIE. Sand poured into the recesses of the wreck and the TIE started to sink into the hole its impact had made. Finn leapt free before the quicksand could claim him, too.

Yes, Finn. *Finn* was his name now.

Watching the TIE vanish into the sand, Finn called out his friend's name one last time. He wished he could have saved Poe's life again.

Finn was still alive, though after a day or two under Jakku's sun, that wouldn't be the case. Stormtrooper training had taught him how to fight in the desert, not how to live in it.

'I don't – know what – to do!' he cried out in anger.

His yell died without so much as an echo. He was alone, but probably not for much longer. The First Order would have tracked the TIE's trajectory and would send troops. Either Finn took his chances with them or with the desert.

Finn chose the desert.

He strode out in a random direction, shedding his armour as he went and holding up Poe's jacket as shade. If the universe had any sort of compassion, perhaps he'd stumble across a settlement or drinking hole before Jakku became his grave.

Rey wove a confusing path through Niima Outpost's marketplace. BB-8 rolled with her and never complained. But after they'd put enough distance between themselves and Unkar Plutt, the droid started to gush with beeps.

She bent down to his level. 'You're welcome for not selling you.' The droid didn't let up singing her praises. 'OK, stop thanking me. I can't help you if you don't tell me who you're waiting for.'

What BB-8 chirped next was far from grateful. Rey rose, insulted. 'Can you *trust* me? What do you think?'

The droid nudged her leg and tweedled something

that wasn't just an apology. She huffed. 'You're waiting for your master. Who?'

BB-8 chirped, and squeaked out a one-syllable name. 'Poe?'

The droid whirled around, sent into a tizzy. After a few rotations, he halted and began to quiz her about her knowledge of galactic history.

'Yes, I know what the Rebellion was – and yes, I've heard of the Resistance.' She frowned when the droid mentioned another faction. 'The First Order? They're horrible. Rumour has it an attack squadron of theirs destroyed the sacred village close to here.'

The droid described the attack with such detail that Rey was appalled. 'You were there?'

BB-8 quit beeping. Shadows on the ground alerted Rey to two hoodlums wrapped in smelly rags coming at them.

'Plutt wants droid,' said one. 'We take droid. Female don't interfere.'

Rey stood her ground. 'The droid's mine. I didn't sell him. Plutt knows that.'

The other stepped in front of Rey. 'You are right. Plutt knows that. You didn't sell. So he take.'

The thug held Rey in place while his partner threw a sack over a screeching BB-8.

Kylo Ren strode across the *Finalizer*'s command bridge. Around him, junior officers and technicians operated an array of equipment, scanning, searching and sifting through vast quantities of data. He paid them no attention, and they, with a shudder, gladly ignored him.

Ren approached General Hux and Captain Phasma, who were analysing the holographic personnel records of a stormtrooper. FN-2187 had no previous offences on his record. He superseded the norms on all his combat readiness tests, both physical and psychological, for the previous mission. From all indications, FN-2187 seemed to be the model stormtrooper.

So what had gone wrong with him, Phasma and Hux wondered aloud. Was his training to blame?

'Finding the flaw in your training methods won't help recover the droid,' Ren said, joining them.

General Hux did not take his eyes off the holofile. 'There are larger concerns than recovering that droid.'

'Not for me,' Ren said.

The general snorted. 'What the Supreme Leader made clear was that the Resistance must not acquire the map to Skywalker. Capture the droid if we can – but *destroy* it if we must.'

Under no circumstances did Ren want the droid destroyed. He needed the BB unit intact to find

Skywalker. But he couldn't disclose that to Hux, because then the general would ensure his soldiers destroyed the droid, just to spite Ren.

'But how capable are your soldiers? They are obviously skilled at high treason,' Ren remarked, casting a glance at the holofile for FN-2187. 'Perhaps the Supreme Leader should consider using a clone army.'

Hux glared at Ren. 'Careful. I won't have you questioning my methods. My men are exceptionally trained, programmed from birth—'

'Have you reviewed the scans of Jakku?' Ren asked. 'Because I believe the droid is likely hidden among the wreckage at Niima Outpost.'

'We found the traitor's armour – a trail in the desert, single tracks, headed towards Niima.' Hux glanced at Captain Phasma, who was standing, silent, next to him. 'A strike team is en route.'

'Good,' Ren said. 'Then I leave it to you, General. To retrieve the droid, *unharmed*.'

He strode off the bridge, relishing the fear he felt emanating from all those he passed.

Water.

Finn saw water. It didn't matter that it was in a trough or that a squat, four-legged happabore was drinking it. All that mattered was that it was water.

He'd trekked across the desert and made it to a

settlement – Niima Outpost, a sign had read. Yet until that water went down his throat, Finn refused to admit anything around him was real. He could be lost in his own desert daydream, his surroundings a mirage. Thirst made people crazy.

Finn dipped his hands into the trough and brought the water to his lips. Nothing had looked so refreshing in his whole life. He drank.

The water went down his throat – and then came back up. Gagging, he spit it out. Nothing had tasted so disgusting in his whole life.

The happabore bumped into Finn, causing him to fall over. Smacking the road made Finn realise that the place was no mirage.

Getting back onto his feet, he saw something in the outpost's bazaar that made him momentarily forget his thirst. Two brutes in grubby rags were assaulting a young woman who looked only a few years younger than Finn.

But the closer Finn got, the more it seemed that the young woman was assaulting *them*.

She pivoted, leapt, and somehow brought down the thug who had tried to pin her in place. The other ruffian dropped the sack he held and rushed her. He should have picked a fight with someone bigger. Drawing her staff from her back, she clubbed and kicked him into submission. By the time Finn reached her, both thugs were knocked out cold.

Wanting to help, and a bit curious, Finn removed the sack from whatever these brutes had wanted to steal. The droid that rolled out astonished him.

It was a BB astromech unit. Orange and white. *One of a kind*, he recalled Poe saying.

He had found Poe's droid.

He also found the girl's staff swinging at his head.

Finn ducked, shouting an objection, but she did not stop. Knowing he was in no condition to fight, he ran, cutting a path of chaos through the marketplace. Merchants cursed him as he toppled shelves and stalls, spilling their wares.

Glancing back and not seeing her, he slowed, believing himself free – until his chest collided with her staff. He lacked the energy to do anything except crumple to the ground.

She loomed over him, brandishing her weapon. 'What's your hurry, thief?'

Before Finn could explain himself, the BB unit spun over and zapped him with its electro-arm. Finn yelped.

'The jacket.' She poked her staff into his arm. 'This droid says you stole it.'

Finn wanted water and shade, not to waste his breath talking about a jacket. 'Listen, I don't want to fight with you. I've already had a pretty messed-up day. So I'd appreciate it if you didn't accuse me of being a thief—' He got zapped again. 'Ow! Stop it!'

'How'd you get it?' She prodded him harder with her staff. 'It belongs to his master.'

Finn looked over at the BB unit, somewhat concerned about what the electro-arm would do when he told the truth. 'His master's dead,' Finn said.

The droid's radar eye stared at him, but the electro-arm remained uncharged.

'His name was Poe Dameron . . . right?' The droid did not answer. Finn addressed the girl. 'He was captured by the First Order. I helped him escape.'

'So you're with the Resistance?' the young woman asked.

Finn glanced at the metal staff that could still club him unconscious. 'Obviously,' he lied. 'I'm with the Resistance . . . yes, I am.'

The young woman seemed to believe him. She swung her staff away from him to point at the droid. 'Beebee-Ate says he's on a secret mission. Says he needs to get back to the nearest Resistance base.'

Finn turned back to the droid and remembered what Poe had told him. 'Apparently he's carrying a map that leads to Luke Skywalker, and everyone's insane to get their hands on it.'

'I thought Luke Skywalker was just a myth.'

Finn almost laughed. 'Really?'

BB-8 broke his mournful silence with a panicked squawk. 'What is it?' the girl asked. 'Over there?' She took a few steps for a better view. Finn stood and followed.

The thugs who had attacked her earlier had regained consciousness and were conversing with two stormtroopers. A meaty arm motioned in their general vicinity.

Finn snatched the young woman's hand and began to backpedal through the bazaar. 'Hey!' she yelled. 'What do you think you're doing?'

'Beebee-Ate, come on!' Finn called out.

The droid did as instructed, seconds before blaster bolts pitted the area where they'd been standing. Pulling the girl with him, Finn caused even more chaos in the bazaar. Merchants cursed him again as he overturned stalls they had just rearranged.

'Let go of me!' The young woman wrested her hand free. But she didn't knock Finn flat with it. Instead she pointed towards a building. 'This way!'

They hurried into a tent that appeared to be used as storage. A pile of salvage provided them cover, but Finn found nothing in it that he could use as an adequate weapon.

Just when it sounded like the troopers had run past and they were safe, BB-8 raised an alarm and zipped to the back of the structure. Finn grabbed the girl's hand again to follow.

'Stop taking my hand!'

Her voice was the last thing he heard before the front of the tent exploded.

The shockwave hurled Rey off her feet, and all of a sudden she was eating dirt. She spit it out and lifted herself off the ground. Through the partially collapsed ceiling, she glimpsed TIE fighters screaming overhead, raining laser fire on all of Niima Outpost.

She looked over at the young man who claimed he was part of the Resistance. He lay facedown on the ground, unmoving. He must have been telling her the truth. The First Order didn't send starfighters after common criminals.

She went to the young man and turned him over. He remained unconscious for a moment, and then his eyes opened. He spoke first. 'Are you OK?'

'Yeah, I'm OK.' She stretched out her hand. He looked at it, then took it. But she quickly let go once she had helped him up. 'Follow me.'

What was left of Niima Outpost burned and smoked. Laser fire had set tents aflame and turned hovels once beloved as homes into rubble. And there was more to come. The two TIE fighters circled back for another strafing run. Merchants, scavengers and townsfolk alike trampled over one another, searching for a place to hide. Rey slid her staff through her back straps and led the young man and BB-8 to a place where no one else was going – a clearing that was the town's starport. Surrounding it were a few grounded starships covered in tarps to protect their components from sandstorms.

Rey sprinted under an archway and across the airfield, with BB-8 and the young man keeping pace. But he was clearly perplexed by her decision and glanced back at the TIEs streaking in their direction. 'Isn't there any shelter around here? We can't outrun them!'

She indicated a vehicle parked at the airfield's edge. 'We might in that quadjumper.'

The young man dismissed it outright. 'I'm a gunner. We need a pilot.'

'We have one,' Rey said confidently.

'You?' His skepticism was something she'd be sure to make him regret.

He pointed at a dilapidated, disc-shaped Corellian freighter that was one of Plutt's personal clunkers. 'How about that ship? It's closer – and if nothing else, we can get out of sight.'

'That one's garbage. We need something that'll move, not just get off the ground,' Rey said.

A barrage from the TIEs blew the quadjumper apart, raining the landing area with metal.

'The garbage'll do!' Rey said.

They veered and ran up the boarding ramp of the freighter. On a whim, Rey tried the controls on the other side of the hatch. To her surprise, the ramp drew back and the hatch closed. Maybe this hunk of junk wasn't quite as junky as it looked.

She and BB-8 headed to the cockpit, where she ditched her staff and plopped down in the pilot's seat.

She flipped a switch on the console and the controls illuminated. A little dusty, perhaps, but perfectly readable.

'Gunner's position is down below,' she called to the young man.

'You ever fly this thing?' he shouted back.

'Nobody's flown this crate in years.'

She initiated the launch sequence. Nothing happened. The engines remained cold. Then she noticed an aftermarket pump had been rigged to the fuel line. She primed the pump and reinitiated the sequence. The engines blazed to life.

'I can do this, I can do this,' she told herself. Strangely, she could've sworn she heard the young man say the same.

The underside repulsors clicked on and lifted the freighter out from under its tarp. But its return to flight was nearly short-lived. It whirled to starboard and dipped, knocking over the archway to the airfield and toppling a vaporator. Only at the last instant did Rey get the control yoke unstuck, avoiding a fiery crash.

She pulled back on the yoke. The freighter rose into the sky, roaring with new life.

In the town below, she saw Unkar Plutt crouch out of his ruined booth and shake his fist at the ship.

But he was the least of her concerns. The two TIEs banked away from Niima Outpost and pursued them.

CHAPTER
8

FINN tried to get comfortable in the gun turret. The controls resembled those shown on broadcasts for classic starship collectors. There were plenty of nifty gauges and switches, but nowhere could he find an ON button. The Corellian freighter was a genuine antique.

But it could fly – boy, this baby could fly. Finn felt the power of the engines thrumming through the conduits of the ship. Niima Outpost quickly disappeared, replaced by dunes of sand. Whether the freighter was fast enough to outrace the two First Order TIEs remained to be seen.

'Stay low,' he said into his headset mic, 'and put up the shields – if they work!'

The girl's voice crackled in his earpiece. 'Not so easy without a copilot!'

Finn swung back and forth in the turret, getting dizzy. The seat's gyros were so loose that even a wiggle would swivel it. 'Try sitting in this thing!'

'Hold on! I'm going low!' she replied.

Low she went, plunging the freighter towards the desert, then pulling up and slowing to skim the surface. They flew so close they lopped off the tops of a couple of sand dunes. The TIEs zoomed over them to avoid a crash, raining down fire with their cannons.

Luckily, Finn's new acquaintance had gotten the shields up in time. Laser fire sizzled and died before it could damage the freighter.

'You ever gonna fire back?' her voice rang in his earpiece.

'Working on it!' He pressed every button and toggled every switch. He didn't know what did it, but the targeting computer suddenly came online.

Holding the triggers in his hands, Finn fired the quad lasers at the TIEs.

All his shots missed.

The TIEs looped to attack. He continued to fire, having no luck. 'We need cover! Quick!'

'We're about to get some,' the girl commed back.

Her idea of cover concerned Finn. She steered the freighter towards what could only have been a former war zone. Demolished vehicles and starships spread out for kilometres, forming a terrifying obstacle course where one wrong turn meant certain death.

Finn kept his fingers on the triggers – and his shots finally connected. A random burst pierced a gap in one of the TIE's shields and took out a wing. The starfighter smashed into the hull of a wrecked capital ship.

Finn let out a cheer. 'That was lucky!'

'Nice shot!' the young woman said.

Their celebration didn't last long. The other TIE unleashed a barrage that hammered the freighter's shields. The impact rocked Finn in his seat and jammed the turret in place. He couldn't swivel, meaning he couldn't target – he could only fire.

'Cannons are stuck in the forward position,' he said. 'I can't move 'em – so you gotta lose 'em!'

The young woman tried to shake their pursuer by diving into the centre engine thruster of an Imperial Super Star Destroyer. All of a sudden they were speeding through a tight maze of shattered beams and crumpled walls. 'Are we really doing this?' Finn asked in disbelief.

'Get ready!' she commed.

'Ready for what?'

The narrow confines hadn't scared off the TIE. Its pilot tracked every move they made and pelted the freighter with lasers.

After a quick climb, they broke out of the destroyer into blue skies. Finn lurched in his harness when the young woman decelerated and cranked the freighter around to face their pursuer. The enemy fighter emerged from the destroyer, dead centre in Finn's crosshair. She had lined up his target for him. All he had to do was fire. Which he did.

The TIE exploded, its own lasers falling well short.

Finn sighed with relief as the freighter soared up and away from the planet Jakku.

Rey put the ship on autopilot and checked on BB-8. The wild ride had pitched the little droid around the cockpit like a kernpop in a kettle. He beeped that he would need 1.3 standard minutes to calibrate his servos.

Rey went into the lounge, where the young man sat near the holochess table, a big grin on his face. 'Now that was *some* flying. How'd you do that?'

'Thanks,' she said. 'But I . . . I'm not sure.'

'Wait – no one trained you?' he asked.

She shook her head. He seemed stupefied. *'No one?'*

'I've flown smaller ships, but I've never left the planet.' She didn't mention that most of those 'ships' had been virtual vessels in her flight simulator.

'Well, that was amazing.' His grin got even bigger. 'You set me up.'

'That last shot was dead on,' she said. 'You got him with one blast.'

He nodded, impressed with himself. 'I know, that was pretty good.'

She laughed. 'It was perfect!'

For a few moments, everything was perfect. Rey

had given Unkar Plutt his comeuppance. She'd escaped soldiers and pilots aiming to kill her. And she'd found a new friend who, unlike BB-8, was flesh and blood. In fact, after getting a good look at him, he was quite—

He cut into her thoughts. 'Why are we—'

'Staring at each other?'

'Yeah,' he said.

'I don't know.'

Fully calibrated, BB-8 spun into the lounge in a blizzard of beeps. Rey touched his sphere, calming him. 'Hey, you're OK, we're OK. He's with the Resistance and he's going to get you home. We both will.'

She looked at her gunner, just now realising the obvious. 'I don't know your name.'

'Eff-Enn-Two—' he started to say. But he corrected himself. 'Finn. What's yours?'

'My name is Rey.'

''Rey,'' he repeated. She liked how he said it.

A pop and a hiss delayed any further introduction. A decking plate had burst loose and gas was venting out. Rey ran over to the hole. 'Quick – help me!'

Finn hurried up beside her. 'What's going on?'

She peered down but couldn't see through the cloud of vapour. 'I don't know. I just hope it's not the motivator!' Covering her eyes, she slipped into the hole.

———

Kylo Ren stared out into the darkness of space from the *Finalizer*'s bridge. Most of the crew were in their quarters, resting. But Ren could not sleep. Not when something so critical was almost in his grasp.

The officer on duty, Lieutenant Mitaka, approached. The man's footsteps were tentative, as if he might run away at any moment. 'Sir,' he said, his voice shaky. 'We were unable to acquire the droid on Jakku. It escaped capture on a stolen Corellian YT-model freighter.'

Ren turned from the observation port. 'The droid stole a freighter?'

'Not exactly, sir. It had help. We had no confirmation, but we believe Eff-Enn-Two-One-Eight-Seven may have been—'

Ren yanked his lightsaber hilt off his belt and ignited its beam. He held the blade overhead. Mitaka closed his eyes.

But it was not the lieutenant Ren struck. Instead he brought down his lightsaber on everything else around him. Slicing through consoles. Tearing open walls. Slashing holes in the deck floor.

When his fury was spent, Ren deactivated his blade and put it back on his belt. 'Anything else?'

Mitaka swallowed. 'The two were accompanied by a girl.'

Like fuel touched by a spark, Ren's rage roared anew. He grabbed Mitaka's throat and squeezed. 'What girl?'

Poe Dameron had died. Or at least he felt that way.

He hobbled along a salt flat in Jakku's desert, sunburnt to a crisp without his flight jacket. His body ached, bruised and cut all over. To either side of him rose hills of sand, sculpted into sharp crests. Sometimes they provided shade, but often the windswept grit stung his eyes and further dried out his mouth. The only good thing he could take from it all was that he remained in the realm of the living. Barely.

He didn't know how long he'd been stumbling through the dunes or how far he'd walked. He had a dim recollection of hitting his head after a barrage of enemy fire bounced him about in the TIE fighter cockpit. When he had awoken, he'd found himself on a collision course with a planet. His instincts took over and he pulled up on the yoke. The action slowed the TIE's descent enough that he could crash-land it and survive. Fearing that the fuel tanks might blow, he crawled out of the vessel immediately. His flight jacket snagged on a crumpled metal edge, forcing him to leave it behind.

But it hadn't been just him in that cockpit. There'd been another. A stormtrooper. One whom Poe had given a name.

'Finn . . . ?' Poe called. 'Finn . . . Finn!'

Of course there was no answer. There wasn't even an echo. The sands muffled his cries.

Most likely Finn had ejected from the TIE. Depending on where and when he launched, he could be kilometres or mere metres away. Poe would probably never know.

He also would probably never know the fate of his astromech droid, BB-8. But if any being was wily enough to get off of Jakku, it was that little mechanical marvel. BB-8 would compute a way to finish the mission. Poe had faith that would happen.

Poe didn't have much faith that he'd be able to do the same. The sun beat down on him. He licked the sweat from around his mouth and kept walking.

CHAPTER
9

IT WAS the motivator.

Finn stood over the hole in the lounge floor and supplied Rey with hydrospanners, Harris wrenches and other tools he couldn't name that she needed to make the repairs. She had sealed most of the gas leaks, but she was still working.

'How bad is it?' he shouted down.

'If we want to live – not good!' she yelled back.

'They're hunting for us. We gotta get out of this system – now!' Finn said.

She popped her head out of the deck hole. 'Beebee-Ate said the location of the Resistance base is on a "need to know" basis. If I'm going to take you two, I need to know.' She went back down to continue banging away at the motivator.

Finn needed to know, too. He pressed the droid to tell him, because the Resistance base was perhaps the only place where the First Order wouldn't be able to kill him.

Unfortunately, what Finn understood from the astromech's tones was that BB-8 didn't trust him – in a big way.

'You just accused me of not being with the Resistance, didn't you?' Finn asked.

The droid tilted up and down in an approximation of a nod.

Finn regarded the odd round droid. Poe had been willing to risk his life to go back for BB-8, a sign that he probably could be trusted with what Finn was about to reveal. 'OK, between us, no I'm not. I'm just trying to get away from the First Order,' he whispered so Rey wouldn't overhear. 'But tell us where your base is, and I'll help you get there first. Deal?'

BB-8's radar eye stared at Finn, but his loudspeaker remained silent.

Rey appeared again. 'Pilex driver, hurry!' While Finn went over to the storage container, she addressed the droid. 'So where's your base?'

The droid stayed quiet. Finn scrounged for the tool. 'Go on, Beebee, tell her.'

The droid shifted his eye back and forth, then finally murmured something short.

'The Ileenium system?' Rey asked.

Finn found the pilex driver and handed it to her. 'The Ileenium system, that's the one.' He tried to sound as if he'd known it all along. 'Let's get there as fast as we can, huh?'

'If I get the ship working again, I'll drop you two off at Ponemah Terminal, but that's as far as I can go.'

'What about you?'

Rey looked at him as if he'd asked a stupid question. 'I gotta get back to Jakku.'

'Back to Jakku? Why does everyone always want to go back to Jakku?'

The flicker of the freighter's interior lights made discussion about Jakku moot.

It wasn't the motivator.

Rey discovered that what was causing their present problem was worse. Much worse.

The cockpit console was dead. All controls were overridden. The engines had gone cold, the lights dimmed, the ship's weaponry was frozen. Someone had taken remote control of the freighter and paralysed it.

Rey sat in the pilot's seat, feeling paralysed herself. She stared out the canopy and saw nothing but space. An unshakable tractor beam emitted from a massive spacecraft was pulling them from the rear.

Returning from the observation port, Finn sank into the copilot's chair. 'It's the First Order.'

The First Order. It hadn't been anything other than

a rumour and a name to Rey until that day. 'What do we do? There must be something—'

'Die,' Finn said.

Rey tried the console again, without luck. 'There have to be other options besides die!'

The freighter creaked as the tractor beam dragged it into its captor's hangar. Everything seemed lost until Finn proposed an idea. Since she couldn't think of anything better, she agreed.

They grabbed breath masks from the lockers, then stowed themselves and BB-8 under the deck in the lounge. Finn slid the plate back over them where it had popped loose. Rey began to pry off the seal she had used to plug the gas leak. 'You sure this will work on the stormtroopers?'

'Their masks filter out smoke, not toxins,' Finn said.

'You Resistance guys really know your stuff.'

Finn grimaced, which struck her as odd. She had intended that to be a compliment.

The freighter's lights suddenly brightened. A clank echoed as the boarding ramp extended. 'They're coming!' Finn said.

Rey could hear the stormtroopers boarding. She didn't have enough time to break the seal she'd tightened moments before *not* to leak. Which meant she wouldn't be able to release the gas to pacify the stormtroopers.

All they could do now was keep quiet and hope the troopers forgot to check for hidden compartments.

———

The pair who came aboard the *Millennium Falcon* were not stormtroopers, but smugglers. One was old, human and somewhat scruffy-looking. The other was almost a half-metre taller and much hairier. They entered the freighter with a measure of fondness and caution, as it had been a long time since they'd walked down her corridors.

The wall paint was chipped in more places than they remembered. Sand had scoured the floors, and many conduits were exposed. The ship had aged, but so had they. And given all that had happened in between, the freighter in which they'd traversed the galaxy didn't look much different from the day they'd last seen her.

'Chewie,' the old man said, 'we're home.'

His first mate – more a term of affection than any distinction of rank – gave a jubilant roar. Chewbacca was a Wookiee, a tall, shaggy-haired species who had the strength to pull arms out of sockets but also the intelligence to engineer the most advanced technologies. Years before, Han Solo had saved Chewbacca's life, and from then on Wookiee custom had bonded Chewbacca to his rescuer, whether the young man liked it or not.

That young man wasn't so young anymore. His hair had greyed. The wrinkles on his face matched the creases in his flight jacket. But Han Solo was far from ready to give up his ghost anytime soon – especially when, after years of searching, he'd finally reunited with the only starship he had ever loved, the *Millennium Falcon*.

Her current operators weren't hard to find. A deck plate in the lounge wasn't flush with the floor. Chewbacca tore it free and Han pointed his blaster at two youths – a male and female, both human – and a newfangled round-modeled droid. The youths raised their hands in surrender.

'Where are the others?' Han asked 'Where's your pilot?'

'I'm . . . the pilot,' the girl stammered.

'*You?*' Han could scarcely believe that someone so young could fly a freighter as highly modified – and uniquely temperamental – as the *Falcon*.

'It's just us. Finn, Beebee-Ate and me,' the girl said.

Chewbacca stomped up next to Han and growled a question. 'No, it's true,' the girl replied. 'We're the only ones on board.'

Finn's eyes widened at her. 'You can *understand* that thing?'

'And 'that thing' can understand you, so watch it,' Han retorted. 'Get outta there.'

The two climbed out of the hole with the droid.

Han gave the girl another curious look. 'Where'd you find the ship?'

'Niima Outpost,' she said.

'Jakku? That junkyard?'

'Thank you!' Finn glanced at the girl, as if to prove a point. 'Junkyard!'

'Told ya we should've double-checked the Western Reaches,' Han said to Chewbacca. They'd been passing through the system in their cargo hauler, with scant interest in Jakku, when the hauler's sensors had detected a familiar beacon – that of the *Falcon*. 'Who had it? Ducain?'

'I stole it from Unkar Plutt,' the girl said.

'Who?'

She lowered her hands. 'He stole it from the Irving Boys, who stole it from Ducain.'

'Who stole it from *me*!' snapped Han. 'You tell him Han Solo just stole back the *Millennium Falcon* for good.'

Both youths dropped their jaws in awe. Han holstered his sidearm and went with Chewbacca to visit the cockpit he hadn't seen in far too long.

CHAPTER
10

HAN SOLO. The *Millennium Falcon*. Though Rey knew little about the First Order, she knew everything about Solo and his famous ship. She'd heard stories of his adventures from traders at Niima and had practised his legendary manoeuvres on her flight simulator.

Rey hurried alongside the old man. 'This is the *Millennium Falcon*? You're Han Solo?'

He smiled crookedly. 'Used to be.'

BB-8 rolled behind while Finn caught up to them, adding his own questions. 'Han Solo? The Rebellion general?'

'No,' Rey said, 'the smuggler!'

Finn seemed baffled. 'Wasn't he a war hero?'

Rey recalled the power she'd felt when overthrusting the engines on Jakku. It all made sense. 'This is the ship that made the Kessel Run in fourteen parsecs.'

'Twelve,' Han insisted. He dismissed her number with a snort. 'Fourteen.' But he sounded more insulted when he read a display in the cockpit. 'Hey – some moof-milker put a compressor on the ignition line!'

Rey and the others joined him in the cockpit. 'Unkar Plutt did. I thought it was a mistake, too, puts too much stress—'

'—on the hyperdrive,' Han said, finishing her sentence. He locked eyes with her. His wrinkles made his expression hard to read. Was he annoyed with her? Or impressed?

Annoyed it seemed, from what he said to his partner. 'Chewie, put 'em in a pod and send them to the nearest inhabited planet.'

'Wait . . . no . . . we need your help!' Rey looked at BB-8. 'This droid has to get to the Resistance base as soon as possible! He's carrying a map to Luke Skywalker.'

The name had an immediate effect on Han. The harsh lines of his wrinkles softened. His gaze grew distant. He became, in Rey's view, just a sad old man.

'You are *the* Han Solo who fought with the Rebellion?' Finn inquired. 'You knew him.'

'Knew him?' Han drew a long breath. 'Yeah . . . I knew Luke.'

A loud clank from the hauler echoed into the *Falcon*'s cockpit. The haze vanished from Han's features, and the hardiness returned. 'Don't tell me a rathtar's gotten loose,' he muttered.

'Wait – a what?' Finn asked.

Han and the Wookiee hastened out of the cockpit.

Rey refused to be left behind, as did Finn and BB-8. They followed the smugglers down the *Falcon*'s boarding ramp into the cargo bay of Solo's hauler.

Finn kept up the questions as Han and Chewbacca kept up the pace through the cargo vessel's main corridor. 'You're not hauling rathtars?'

'I'm hauling rathtars.'

Entering the larger vessel's primary hold, Han keyed one of the many consoles. A three-dimensional hologram of the cargo hauler materialised, showing a smaller, needle-nosed ship attached to it. 'It's the Guavian Death Gang. They must've tracked us from Nantoon.' The Wookiee groaned. 'That's never good. I hate that.'

'What?' Finn asked.

'When someone who wants to kill us finds us.' Han and Chewbacca hustled out of the cockpit, forcing Finn, Rey and BB-8 to follow down the corridor again.

Rey finally had a chance to ask Finn her burning question. 'What's a rathtar?'

Finn turned to her. 'Ever heard of the Trillia Massacre?'

'No.'

'Good,' he said.

'I got three going to King Prana,' Han bragged.

'Three!' Finn shook his head.

Rey ignored him. 'How'd you get them aboard?'

'Let's just say I used to have a bigger crew.'

Stopping in the corridor, Han pressed a concealed

button on the bulkhead. A section of the floor retracted, revealing a step ladder. 'Get below deck until I say so.'

'What about Beebee-Ate?' Rey asked.

'He'll stay with me,' Han said. 'When I get rid of the gang, you can have him back and be on your way.'

Finn waited until Rey descended the ladder. 'The rathtars . . . where are you keeping them?'

A tremendous boom shook the corridor. Behind a thick transparisteel port in the corridor's wall clacked a circular row of teeth large enough to chew a Wookiee.

Han chuckled. 'Well, there's one.'

The creature rammed the port again.

'Now get below!' Han told Finn.

Finn quickly did just that. Rey stepped back to look up at Han. 'What are you going to do?'

'Same thing I always do,' he said to her. 'Talk my way out of it.'

Chewbacca rolled his eyes and groaned.

Rey watched Han and Chewbacca hotfoot it down the corridor, arguing with each other the entire way. BB-8 rolled after them, with nary a beep. His radar eye looked back at Rey, and then the floor hatch closed.

Han, Chewbacca and BB-8 hadn't gone far down the corridor when they encountered their uninvited guests. A portal irised open and out stepped six members of the Guavian Death Gang. Five were security goons armed with percussive cannons and clad in mottled scarlet uniforms with black leg greaves and shoulder pauldrons. A dark circle marked the centre of their polished red helmets. No spot of colour showed on the leather coat and heavy boots of the sixth Guavian, their leader. He wore no helmet, exposing brown hair and a face that looked too boyish for a life of crime. The percussive cannon he aimed at Han and Chewbacca said otherwise.

'I got this, leave it to me,' Han whispered to his partner. Chewbacca snorted, as he always did when Han took the lead. It wouldn't be the same if he didn't. It was all part of their routine.

BB-8 took the Wookiee's side and hid behind his hairy leg.

The Death Gang leader advanced towards them. 'Han Solo. You are a dead man.'

Han welcomed him with a grin. 'Bala-Tik. What's the problem?'

Bala-Tik did not grin back. 'The problem is we loaned you fifty thousand for this job.'

'And you're going to profit from it handsomely.'

'You also borrowed fifty thousand from Kanjiklub,' Bala-Tik said.

'Who told you that?'

'Kanjiklub.'

'Oh, come on. You can't trust those little freaks.' Han exhaled, then used his warm and friendly voice again. 'Bala, how long have we known each other?'

'The question is, how much longer will we know each other? Not long, with your excuses,' Bala-Tik said. 'We want our money back. Now.'

'You think it's easy hunting rathtars? I spent that money.'

'Kanjiklub wants their investment back, too.'

'I never made a deal with Kanjiklub!'

'Tell that to Kanjiklub.'

A second portal irised open behind Chewbacca and Han. From it emerged a motley mob of goons, none of whom were little or freakish. Compared with the Guavians, they dressed more like the pirates they were, with eye patches and soiled jerkins, but their various weapons were just as lethal.

Chewbacca snarled when the head of the second boarding party stepped forward. The man had an olive complexion, a knife-thin moustache, and eyes just as sharp. Han hailed him with the same bogus smile he had given Bala-Tik. 'Tasu Leech. Good to see you.'

Leech spit out words in his native tongue, which Han didn't need to be fluent in to understand. The gangster wanted Han and Chewbacca to rot.

Leech raised his bayoneted rifle – but Bala-Tik blocked his line of fire. 'That BB unit,' he said to Han, eyeing the droid. 'The First Order is looking for one just like it. And two fugitives.'

'First I've heard of it,' Han said.

A sudden loud clank seemed to dispute that. Han cringed. What were those kids doing?

Leech's first mate, a despicable rogue whom Han knew as Razoo Qin-Fee, commanded the others to search the freighter.

'Where'd you get the droid?' Bala-Tik demanded.

'He's mine, that's where,' Han said.

'We're going to take the droid,' Bala-Tik declared. 'And our money.'

Razoo repeated Leech's threat, adding that Han could choose whether they took the droid freely or off his dead body.

Then the lights blinked off and on. The constant whir of instrumentation around them was drowned out by an awful racket of snapping and skittering that echoed through the corridor.

'I got a bad feeling about this,' Han muttered.

Finn had a bad feeling about this.

He and Rey had wormed through the service tunnel, reaching a ventilation shaft that permitted them to hear and see some of what was happening in the corridor. Wanting a fuller view, Rey had stepped up on a support beam to peek through the vent. But the beam had cracked under her, making the sound that had alerted the Kanjiklubbers to search for them.

The gangsters were the least of their problems at the moment.

While messing with a fuse box that controlled both the ship's illumination and its blast doors, Rey uttered the dreaded 'uh-oh.' The lights flickered above them, but blast doors did not descend to trap each gang, as intended.

''Uh-oh' what?' Finn asked.

'Wrong fuses,' Rey said.

The terrible noise that followed confirmed that they were, indeed, the wrong fuses. Instead of shutting all the ship's blast doors, they had opened them, thereby releasing what had been locked away.

'Rathtars,' Finn said with a gulp.

He crawled down the tunnel after Rey. Their survival depended on getting as far away as they could from the rathtars – and the *Millennium Falcon* seemed their best bet to do so. Finn wished Han and Chewbacca could join them, but listening to the commotion above, it probably wasn't going to be possible.

'New plan!' the one Han had called Bala-Tik shouted. 'Kill them and take the droid!'

Blasters fired, followed by screams.

Finn winced. He had heard those sounds too frequently within the past day.

Yet the screams continued, in greater volume and

frequency than a pair of smugglers, or even a Wookiee in pain, could ever produce on their own.

The rathtars.

Finn lifted the first access hatch they saw and hoisted himself out. Finding the corridor clear of both men and monsters, he helped Rey climb out, then motioned. '*Falcon's* this way.'

'You sure?'

'No,' he said, but they rushed off in that direction anyway.

'What do these rathtars look like?' Rey asked.

'Horrible,' he said, turning the corner, then back-pedalling immediately. 'They look like that.'

Rey froze, covering her mouth. Around the corner, a round, pulsating, many-tentacled abomination fought a gangster, though it wasn't much of a fight. The gangster's blaster shots did little but glance off the sensory bulbs that covered the carnivore's body, further enraging it. Caught in its tentacles, the man was drawn shrieking into its massive maw of razor teeth.

Finn grabbed Rey and pulled her away to race back down the corridor. But human speed was no match for a rathtar. A tentacle lashed out and entangled Finn.

He fought, he kicked, he bit and he punched. The tentacle's viselike grip only tightened around his waist, dragging him towards the rathtar's mouth. Like the gangster before him, and those poor beings in the Trillia

Massacre, Finn was going to be munched into hundreds of pieces.

He didn't hear his own screams. He only heard Rey calling out his name.

'Finn!'

Rey yelled his name twice as the beast spun around the corner, taking Finn. She ran after it, but once again, it proved too fast, turning another corner. It wanted to enjoy its meal in peace.

She halted, glimpsing a sign on a door. She palmed the door panel and entered the cargo hauler's auxiliary control room.

She went straight for a bank of monitors that showed the interior sections of the ship. One displayed the corridor down which the hideous monster was pulling a still-struggling Finn.

When the rathtar slinked into an intersection, Rey touched the console below the monitors. There were no wrong fuses to trip. There was only a bulkhead blast door to activate. It dropped down to slice through the tentacle that held Finn.

The audio pickups relayed the shriek of the wounded rathtar. But Rey's focus was on the other side of the blast door, where Finn was yanking off clumps of tentacle. She mapped his location and darted out of the control room.

When she found him, he was shaking, breathing hard. 'There was a door . . . it shut . . . precisely at . . .'

'Lucky,' she said.

Taking cover behind a stack of crates, Han could see his baby. The *Millennium Falcon* sat undisturbed at the other end of the cargo bay.

Blaster bolts lit up the air and struck the crates. A group of Guavians and Kanjiklubbers fired at them. Han fired back, as did Chewbacca, kneeling beside Han and wielding his enormous Wookiee bowcaster. BB-8 crammed himself between them, having no defense against this kind of long-range attack.

Han gauged the distance to his ship. It wasn't far. Trouble was, he'd be making himself an easy target for the surviving thugs firing away from the corridor.

Despite the odds, he had to try.

'I'll get the door,' he told Chewie. 'Cover us.'

He jabbed a finger at the droid, signalling him to follow, and then the two were off, racing towards the *Falcon* in direct view of their pursuers. Chewbacca meanwhile spent half his bandolier pumping out plasma quarrel after plasma quarrel at the corridor.

Han and BB-8 made it unscathed to the *Falcon*. Han opened the hatch and the boarding ramp lowered.

He then began to lay down some covering fire of his own. 'Chewie! Come on!'

The Wookiee roared and ran towards the ship, his immense stride covering much of the distance in half the time it had taken Han.

He was not fast enough.

Blaster fire hit Chewbacca in the shoulder. The Wookiee went down.

Letting BB-8 ascend the ramp, Han grabbed Chewie's bowcaster and sprinted back into the firefight. He blasted the Guavian who had dared make that shot, then called on every muscle in his body to lift his heavy friend. Together they staggered towards the *Falcon*, with Han firing at the gangsters.

Han's marksmanship was near perfect. The gangsters' was not. They fell back, losing too many of their number, while Han and Chewie made it to the *Falcon*.

'Han!' shouted a female voice. The two kids dashed across the bay towards them.

'You shut the hatch behind us,' he ordered the girl, then hoisted his friend on Finn. 'You take care of Chewie.'

Finn almost plunged off the ramp under his hairy burden. 'How do I do that?'

Han left Chewie to bark out directions and hastened into the cockpit, where old habits took over. He sat in his well-worn seat and started flipping switches and turning dials to initiate the launch sequence. Though he hadn't done it in years, never once did he hesitate; he knew the *Falcon*'s procedure by heart. Going through it in his head was how Han had coaxed himself to sleep at night.

He almost didn't notice when the girl sat in Chewie's seat. 'Hey! What are you doing?'

She leaned over the copilot's console and pushed a series of buttons. 'Unkar installed a fuel pump, too. If you don't prime it, we're not going anywhere.'

Han glanced at the scopes and gauges. The girl was right. 'I hate that guy.'

'And you can use a copilot.'

Han scoffed. 'I got one. He's back there.'

Chewbacca could be heard yowling in the medbay - though from the sound of it, Han was uncertain whether it was due to pain or sheer irritation at his nurse's attempts to calm him down. 'It's just a flesh wound!' Finn shouted, which only incensed the Wookiee further.

After checking that the girl had indeed primed the fuel pump, Han warmed the engines and set the navicomputer to calculate routes. 'Watch the thrust, we're gonna jump to lightspeed—'

She gave him a look of absolute bewilderment. 'From *inside* a hangar? Is that even possible?'

Han continued to make flight adjustments on his console. 'I never ask a question until after I've done it,' he told the girl. He refrained from conceding that, like her, he wasn't convinced it would work.

They were out of options when a rathtar leapt out of

a corridor and landed atop the ship. Within seconds, it had scurried over the hull to hug the cockpit. The girl shrieked as the creature tried to bite through the canopy to eat them, leaving trails of slime.

'This is not how I thought this day would go,' Han said. 'Angle the shields—'

She tapped her controls. 'Got it!'

'Hang on back there,' Han shouted to his other passengers.

'No problem!' Finn called back.

Han gripped the hyperdrive lever. He gave the navicomputer another second of computation. 'Come on, baby, don't let me down.'

He pulled the lever.

Something whined. They didn't move. The rathtar's teeth continued to chomp against the canopy while the *Falcon* remained steadfastly in the hangar.

'What!' Han said. If Plutt had messed with his hyperdrive, Han would go to Jakku himself and throttle the numbskull.

'Compressor,' the girl said.

Of course – that moof-milker had installed a compressor on the ignition line. Han was about to reach over and switch it on, but the girl did it for him. His glare became a grin, showing her his appreciation.

Han pulled the lever again.

CHAPTER
11

THE *Falcon*'s hasty jump into hyperspace jostled Finn around the medbay, but didn't rip him apart. The wounded Wookiee seemed eager to do that himself. Every time Finn administered an injection or tried to apply a bandage, Chewbacca bellowed and shook Finn with such force that he thought his arms might fly off.

'Chewie, you've got to let go of me, understand? Help me out here!'

The Wookiee grunted, only tightening his grip on Finn. Worse yet, alarms began to wail throughout the ship, making it hard for Finn to think.

He turned towards the doorway and yelled as loud as he could. 'I need help with this fuzzball!'

Han popped into the medbay with a growl of his own. 'You hurt Chewie, you deal with me.'

'Hurt him? He's almost killed me six times!' Finn complained. Chewbacca grabbed his shirt and snarled. 'Which is . . . fine,' Finn stammered.

Han rushed off to deal with the alarms, muttering something about the hyperdrive.

Yet Han's appearance, albeit brief, did much to calm Chewbacca, and Finn managed to bandage the Wookiee's shoulder without losing any limbs.

When the alarms fell silent, Han returned to the medbay. Finn stepped out of the way and started to toy with the holochess set. He listened as Chewbacca groaned something to Han that sounded apologetic.

'No, don't say that. You did great.' Han checked the bandaging. 'You're gonna be fine.' He glanced at Finn. 'Good job. Thanks.'

Surprised by Han's gratitude, Finn hesitated. 'You're welcome.'

Holographic creature chess pieces materialised above the board, making noises of their species types. Embarrassed, Finn searched for the off button. Han seemed amused that Finn couldn't find it. 'So, you're fugitives, huh?'

Finn cocked his head in the direction of BB-8. 'The First Order will kill all of us for that map in the little guy's brain.' His fingers flicked a control and the chess pieces disappeared.

Rey walked in, with a nod towards Finn and the droid. 'They're with the Resistance, and *I'm* with *them*.'

Han looked Finn and Rey over once again, then turned to BB-8. 'Let's see what you got.'

BB-8 rotated a lens on his dome and projected in the air a partial three-dimensional map of the galaxy. Finn gaped at stars, solar systems and nebulae he'd never seen.

Han drew an invisible line through the map. 'This isn't complete. It's just a piece.'

Finn squinted at the map. There were stellar clusters that didn't fit next to each other and dark patches that should be populated with planets and stars.

'Ever since Luke disappeared, people have been looking for him,' Han said.

'Why'd he leave?' Rey asked.

Han hesitated, then let out a breath. 'He was training a new generation of Jedi. One boy – an apprentice – turned against him and destroyed it all.' Han's wrinkles seemed to multiply at the recollection. 'Luke felt responsible. He walked away from everything.'

That wasn't what the First Order had ever told Finn. 'You know what happened to him?'

'There have been all kinds of rumours and stories,' Han said. 'The people who knew him the best think he went looking for the first Jedi Temple.'

Rey looked stunned. 'The Jedi were real?'

'I used to wonder that myself. A bunch of mumbo jumbo, I thought. Some magical power holding together good and evil, light and dark.' Han shook his head and smiled. 'Crazy thing is, it's all real. The Jedi, the Force, it's . . . true. It's all true.'

Finn's brain hurt. His conception of the universe was falling apart. Did the Jedi and the Force actually exist? Had the First Order lied about them, too? Finn doubted a smuggler as seasoned as Han Solo would believe in such myths unless he had seen hard proof that they were real.

What Han said next could not be disputed. He used Finn's own words. 'The First Order will kill all of us for that map.'

Death would be the most merciful outcome, Finn feared, if Kylo Ren was the one to find them.

Kylo Ren stood with General Hux in the cavernous command room of the First Order's hidden military outpost, Starkiller Base. At this off-duty hour, all techs and officers had vacated the chamber, allowing Ren and Hux the privacy to converse with Supreme Leader Snoke. His hologram shimmered before them on an elevated dais, giant in size though he himself was gaunt. He sat on a throne, steepling his spindly fingers. The flesh visible under his robe glowed with a pale pink translucence. Scars marked his forehead and chin, and his nose, once broken, protruded at a painful angle. But most disconcerting was the imbalance of his eyes. They peered out from his hood like two dark stars, his left eye lower than his right.

Shadow veiled the rest of him, which only reinforced the commanding presence of his voice.

'The droid will soon be in the hands of the Resistance,' Snoke said. 'This will give our enemy the means to locate Skywalker and bring to their cause a most powerful ally. If Skywalker returns, the new Jedi will rise.'

Hux lowered his head in deference. 'Supreme Leader, I take full responsibility for the—'

'Your apologies are not a strategy, General. We are here, now. It's what happens next that matters.'

Ren kept quiet, allowing Hux to do the speaking. 'I do have a proposition. The weapon. We have it. It is ready. I believe the time has come to use it.'

'Against?' the Supreme Leader asked.

'The Republic. Their centre of government, its entire system,' Hux said. 'In the chaos that follows, the Resistance will no doubt investigate an attack of such a devastating scale, and in the process—'

'Reveal themselves,' Snoke interjected.

Hux nodded. 'And if they don't, we've destroyed them.'

'Yes ... audacious ... Good. Go,' the Supreme Leader ordered Hux. 'Oversee preparations.'

Hux bowed before the hologram. 'Yes, Supreme Leader.' He walked out of the chamber, leaving Ren alone with the image.

Snoke's voice assumed a fatherly tone. 'I never had a student with such promise . . . before you.'

'It's your teachings that make me strong, Supreme Leader,' Ren said.

'It is far more than that. It is where you are from. What you are made of. The dark side,' the Supreme Leader said, hesitating before saying the next words, 'and the light.'

Ren felt the Supreme Leader's eyes, incorporeal though they were, probing him. 'Kylo Ren,' he went on, 'I watched the Galactic Empire rise and fall. The historians have it wrong. It was neither poor strategy nor arrogance that brought down the Empire. You know, too well, what did.'

Ren spit out the answer as if it were poison. 'Sentiment.'

'Yes. Sentiment,' the Supreme Leader said. 'Had Lord Vader not succumbed to emotion at that critical moment – had the father *killed* the son – there would be no threat of Skywalker's return today.'

Ren understood that the Supreme Leader had brought up Vader to test him. 'I am immune to the light,' Ren said, standing tall and firm.

'There has been an awakening in the Force. Have you felt it?'

'Yes,' Ren said.

'The elements align, Kylo Ren. You alone are caught

in the winds of a powerful storm. Your bond is not just to Vader, but to Skywalker himself. Leia—'

'There is no need for concern. Together we will destroy the Resistance,' Ren assured his master, 'and the last Jedi.'

'Perhaps. The droid we seek is aboard the *Millennium Falcon*, once again piloted by your father, Han Solo. Even you, a master of the Knights of Ren, have not faced such a test.'

Ren did his best to hide his surprise. 'It does not matter. He means nothing to me. By the grace of your training, I will not be seduced.'

Ren bowed and turned to leave, feeling the Supreme Leader's gaze weighing on him well after he had exited the chamber.

Rey stared out the cockpit canopy of the *Millennium Falcon*. The streaks of lightspeed had coalesced into their destination, a single spectacular planet. Beneath a cloud layer sparkled a world of greens and blues. A tangle of lakes and rivers surrounded verdant landforms lush with vegetation. If Jakku had an opposite, Takodana was it.

'I didn't know there was this much green in the whole galaxy,' she said.

Her awe only grew when the *Falcon* landed and she disembarked, taking in an unfiltered view of the environment. An ancient fortress built of stone lay between a glass-clear lake and a dense, vibrant forest.

Han walked down the boarding ramp towards her. He held out a blaster pistol. She glanced at it. 'I've been in tough situations. I can handle myself.'

'That's why I'm giving it to you,' Han said.

She took the blaster. It was an antiquated model, much like the *Falcon*. 'It's heavy.'

'You know how to fire that?'

She smirked at him. 'You aim it and pull the trigger.'

'A bit more to this model. Put a little effort in, get more result out,' Han said. 'You got a name?'

She lifted the weapon and pointed it at her surroundings, practising her aim. 'Rey.'

'Rey,' he said, as if trying it out. 'Rey, I've been thinking about taking on some more crew. A second mate. Someone who can keep up with Chewie and me and who's smart enough to know when to keep out of the way.' His voice lost some of its bite. 'Someone who appreciates the *Falcon*.'

'Are you giving me a job?' she asked.

'It doesn't pay right away. And I'm not going to be nice to you—'

'You're offering me a job.'

'I'm just thinking about it,' Han said.

Rey chose her next words carefully. 'Well . . . if you did, I'd be flattered. But there's somewhere I need to be.'

'Jakku?'

'I've already been away too long,' Rey said.

Han nodded. 'Let me know if you change your mind.' He leaned towards the *Falcon*'s hatch. 'Chewie! Check her out the best you can. We won't be here long.' He pivoted back. 'You smile too much, Rey.'

Rey didn't stop smiling as he walked away.

CHAPTER
12

LEAVING Chewbacca to guard the *Falcon*, Han led Rey, Finn and BB-8 up a flight of stone stairs to the fortress proper. It had been years since he'd been here and seen its owner. He hoped her good opinion of him hadn't changed. Otherwise, they might have been better off with the rathtars.

'Why are we here again?' Finn asked.

'To get your droid on a clean ship. You think it was luck that Chewie and I found the *Falcon*? If we can find it on our scanners, the First Order's not far behind. Want to get BB-8 to the Resistance? Maz Kanata is our best bet. She's run this watering hole for a thousand years. Maz is an acquired taste,' Han told the youths, 'so let me do the talking. And whatever you do, don't stare.'

'At what?' Rey asked.

'Any of it,' Han said gruffly.

At the top of the stairs, they passed through the open gate, then went down a corridor that directed them into a great hall. The place was as rowdy and rough as any cantina Han had ever frequented. At the many tables sat blue-bearded Narquois, chortling Ubdurians and puffy yellow Frigosians. A woman in a black-and-white baffleweave bodysuit sat in the lap of a heavyset Dowutin. Lurching about on a peg leg was a saggy Gabdorin. Three white-furred bipeds Han knew as the Hassk triplets snarled from a corner. Han snarled back. He never showed fear in holes like this. Walking through the throng with the kids, he hurled glares and vicious threats to ward off any would-be aggressors.

There was one whom Han did not insult. Short and slim, she had skin wrinkled like Han's but with the colour of spoiled citrus. The ends of a tightly tied bandana drooped from her bald head, though the rest of her apparel was loose fitting. Gadgets of all sorts dangled from an animal-hide belt around her waist, and rings and bracelets adorned her fingers and wrists. But the most striking features of her person were the scope-sized lenses around each eye – and the voice that shrieked from her tiny mouth.

'Haaaan Sooolo?'

The great hall became so quiet Han could've heard a worm move. 'Hiya, Maz,' he said.

'Under the radar,' Finn whispered. 'Perfect.'

'You still in business?' Han called out to Maz.

'Barely!' she shouted, heading towards them from

across the hall. 'Thanks to a certain mooch who still hasn't paid me back after nearly twenty years.' She reached Han and looked up at him. 'Can you imagine something so horrible?'

Han twitched. 'I might be able to.'

'Where's my boyfriend?' Maz asked.

'Chewie's repairing the *Falcon*.'

'That's one sweet Wookiee.' Maz looked over at Finn and Rey. 'I'm sorry.'

'About what?' Finn asked.

'Whatever trouble he's dragged you into.' Maz turned to Han again. 'Come! Sit! I can't wait to hear what you need from me this time.'

Salvation for Poe Dameron arrived in the form of a rattletrap speeder. It wheezed towards him, a mishmash of refurbished salvage. In his woozy, dehydrated state, Poe had never seen anything more beautiful.

The speeder's pint-sized Blarina driver had scaly skin better suited for Jakku's desert than Poe's, though he still wore garb that covered most of his body, including reflective sunshades over his eyes. He offered Poe a many-toothed smile. 'Enjoying the sunshine?'

'I'm lost,' Poe said.

'Indeed you are. Where'd you leave your speeder?'

'Never had one,' Poe said.

The Blarina clucked his tongue. 'Then I might have to scavenge you.'

'Why would you do that? I'm lost, and it's said that the Blarina are an exceptionally hospitable people.'

The Blarina's snout wrinkled. 'Doesn't sound like me. Must be referring to some other Blarina.'

'Take what you want,' Poe said, opening his arms. 'As you can see, I've got nothing worth scavenging.'

The Blarina lifted his sunshades. His pupil slits glinted gold. 'Then what are you doing out here, with 'nothing'?'

'I escaped from the First Order by stealing one of their TIEs,' Poe said, 'shot up a Star Destroyer, then crash-landed in this sand dump.'

Tipping his head back, the Blarina broke into a cackle and didn't stop for quite some time. 'That's the most ridiculous lie I've ever heard. Absolutely unbelievable,' he said, dabbing away tears. 'Get aboard, my friend.'

The Blarina reached out with five stumpy claws. Poe took hold of his hand and staggered into the speeder. Bunching his knees to his chest, he wedged himself into the passenger's seat that was designed for someone much smaller. 'Might you have any water?'

'Might you have a name, human?'

'Poe. Poe Dameron.'

'Glad to make your acquaintance, Poe Dameron.' The Blarina handed him a metal flask. 'I'm Naka Iit.'

Poe sucked as much water as he could through the flask's siptube. He came up to breathe in between gulps. 'Need . . . to get . . . offworld.'

Naka reset the sunshades over his eyes. 'Course you do. Already have enough madmen on Jakku.' He reengaged the engines and gained some elevation. 'Nearest settlement is Niima Outpost. But I wouldn't take my worst cousin there. It's run by a saggy sleazesack known as Plutt. Only time I'll be seeing him is when they bury that slimemonger. There'll be a fight for who'll drop the first shovel of sand.'

'Is there anywhere else?'

'Know a Blarina trader in Blowback Town called Ohn Gos. He has a soft spot for sob stories. Might be able to get you off Jakku for the right price.'

'I don't have any credits,' Poe said.

'Your problem, not mine. If you don't want to go—'

'Take me there,' Poe said.

Naka accelerated the speeder. The three engines whined in protest, shaking both driver and passenger. Poe thought the whole thing was going to burst apart at any moment. Naka, however, didn't seem concerned.

Blaster fire pelted a nearby dune.

Poe glanced over his shoulder. A speedertruck zoomed towards them. Another eruption from a dune on the opposite side verified their pursuit was not friendly.

Naka growled. 'Strus clan. Pack of no-good thieves want my speeder.'

Poe looked back again. 'Well, they're gonna take it unless we go faster.'

'This ain't a podracer, it's a salvage lugger.'

'I can make it go faster. Give me the yoke.'

'Over my dead molt would I ever—'

Poe's size worked in his favour. He grabbed the control yoke with one hand while pushing the Blarina away with the other. Naka eventually found himself shifted over to Poe's seat while Poe took the driver's position, clamping the yoke with his knees.

Instead of speeding up, Poe slowed down.

'What the grunk are you doing?' Naka popped his sunshades. 'Is this some sort of trick?'

'Gesture we're yielding,' Poe said.

Naka grumbled. 'This is what I get for being hospitable.'

The Blarina stood up and waved with both hands. The speedertruck stopped firing and decelerated. Soon it rode parallel with Poe. The bandits peered down from the truck bed, grinning at their trophy.

Poe smiled back and switched off two of the engines, as if about to park. That never happened. His knees yanked the control yoke down, pointing the speeder towards the sky.

The thrust nozzle blew apart a dune and launched

the speeder upward as if it were a starship. The bandits had no time to react before they were blanketed in a sandstorm. Poe kept taking them into the clouds, well past the specifications for a normal speeder.

Waving at the bandits below, Naka began to cackle again. Their pursuers couldn't attain any lift, since sand and salt had plugged their truck's repulsors. 'You must be with the Resistance,' he said to Poe. 'No one else would try something so crazy.'

'"Courageous" is the word we prefer,' Poe replied.

'Call it what you want, madness is madness.' Naka clawed grit out of his teeth. 'But my speeder's all I have, and you saved it.'

'See what being hospitable gets you?'

Naka hissed through his snout. 'Don't press your luck. I'll put in a word with Ohn Gos, and we'll get you off Jakku. But that's the limit of Naka Iit's hospitality.'

'It's good enough for me. Thank you.'

'Thank me all you want, but the truth is, the farther away from your lunatic antics that I am, the safer I feel.'

Poe laughed for the first time since he had accepted his mission.

Finn ate his fill of the feast Maz served them, but Rey gorged. He watched the slender girl scarf down anything and everything served on the long tiled table, as if it might be taken away at a moment's notice. Taste and appearance did not factor in to what she crammed in her mouth. Getting food into her stomach seemed to be her primary goal. What had she been eating on Jakku? Or perhaps more accurately, what *hadn't* she been eating?

Han regaled Maz with his account of their escape from the Guavians and Kanjiklubbers, conspicuously omitting any mention of the rathtars. Maz grew excited when he spoke of what BB-8 carried. 'A map leading to the first Jedi Temple! To Skywalker himself! I've never given up hope for him.'

'That's good to hear, because I have a favour to ask,' Han said.

Maz cocked her head at Han. 'You need a loan.' Han's grin wavered. 'Yes, I heard about the rathtars.' She looked over at Rey. 'How's the food?'

'Delicious!' Rey said between mouthfuls.

Han gestured at BB-8. 'I need you to get this droid to the Resistance.'

'Me?' Maz asked.

'And the loan sounds good,' Han added.

Maz leaned closer to Han. 'I'll help you find passage and avoid Snoke's hunter squads. But this journey to the Resistance isn't mine to take, and you know it.'

'Leia doesn't want to see me.'

'Who can blame her? But this fight is about more than you and that good woman. Han. Go home,' Maz said firmly.

'What fight?' Rey asked, totally lost.

'The only fight: against the dark side. Through the ages, I've seen evil take many forms. The Sith. The Empire. Today, it is the First Order. Their shadow is spreading across the galaxy. We must fight them. All of us.'

'That's crazy,' Finn said. 'Look around. There's no chance we haven't been recognised already. I bet the First Order is on their way right—' He stopped talking when he noticed Maz adjusting her goggles, making her eyes appear even larger. 'Solo, what's she doing?'

'No idea,' Han said, 'but it ain't good.'

Maz climbed up onto the table and walked over to directly in front of Finn. 'If you live long enough, you see the same eyes in different people. I'm looking at the eyes of a man who wants to run.'

'You don't know a thing about me,' Finn snapped. 'Where I'm from. What I've seen. You don't know the First Order like I do. They'll slaughter us. We all need to run.' He got to his feet. 'I'm out.'

Rey's brow furrowed in shock. 'What?'

'I need to get to the Outer Rim, right now,' Finn said, ignoring her.

Maz gestured through the doorway to a table in the great hall. 'Big head, red shirt, shiny gun. Bright red helmet with ear flares. They're bound for the Outer Rim. Will trade transportation for work. Go,' she commanded.

Finn looked at Rey. She wouldn't meet his gaze. He stood, unholstered his blaster and handed it to Han. 'It's been nice knowing you. Really was.'

Han wouldn't meet his gaze, either, or take the pistol. 'Keep it.'

There were no more words exchanged. It seemed anticlimactic after all they had been through. But that was the life of a soldier. You got close to people during intense situations, then the next thing you knew, you were heading off in different directions.

Finn's direction would be any civilised world far from the First Order and the Resistance.

Rey sat at Maz's table, stung by Finn's departure. She had saved his life multiple times, and yet he had dumped her like an empty blaster cartridge. She chided herself for thinking he would be different. If her short life had taught her anything, it was that those close to her would abandon her. That was the way of the galaxy. Best to live alone and look out only for number one. Then you wouldn't get hurt. Then you would survive.

So why did she suddenly find herself going after him?

He was standing at a table in the great hall, asking for a lift from a person dressed in red, with a black cloak around his shoulders and a flared helmet. He must be the starship captain of whom Maz had spoken. The captain might have been human under the costume, for all Rey knew, but his plump, peg-legged lieutenant and the rest of the crew were definitely not.

Rey ignored the aliens' stares and strode right up to Finn. 'What are you doing?'

'Give me a second,' Finn said to the captain. He led Rey away from the table.

She did not allow him a chance to make excuses. 'You heard what Maz said. You're part of this fight. We both are.' As she looked at him up close, her anger abated. She saw a young man as confused and conflicted as she was. 'You must feel something.'

He looked away from her. 'I'm not who you think I am. I'm not . . . special. Not in any way.'

'Finn, what are you talking about? I've watched you. I've seen you in action—'

'I'm a stormtrooper,' Finn said.

His confession confounded her more. He was a stormtrooper? A soldier for the First Order? Was everything she knew about him – *felt* about him – a lie?

'I was taken from a family I'll never know. I was raised and trained to do one thing. Kill my enemy. But my first battle, I made a choice. I wasn't going to kill for them. So I ran. Right into you.' Finn's voice broke, but he quickly recovered. 'You asked me if I was Resistance, and looked at me like no one ever had. I was ashamed of what I was. But I'm done with the First Order. I'm never going back.' He paused. 'Rey, come with me.'

'Don't go,' Rey pleaded.

'Take care of yourself. Please,' Finn said sadly. Without another word, he rejoined the captain and his crew. Rey turned and walked away so she wouldn't have to see him again.

Kylo Ren was angry.

Angry at General Hux and his crew for allowing the freighter to escape. Angry at himself for not trusting his feelings about a trooper he'd seen on Jakku. Angry that the Supreme Leader would even consider that he, Kylo Ren, could be turned to the light.

He knelt in his dark chambers aboard the Star Destroyer. Though he was alone, he spoke in a low and respectful tone. 'Forgive me. I feel it again. The pull to the light. The Supreme Leader senses it. Show me again the power of the darkness, and I will let nothing stand in our way. Show me, Grandfather, and I will finish what you started.'

The shrine's centrepiece was a symbol that once was feared throughout the galaxy. Flames had warped and melted it into a shape even more monstrous than before. Though cool to the touch, evil emanated from it as if it continued to burn.

It was the relic of a dead man to whom Kylo Ren felt a dark kinship.

It was the burnt husk of the mask of Darth Vader.

CHAPTER
13

WHEN Rey returned to Maz's table, Han and the pirate queen were still debating what to do with BB-8. Rey didn't linger. She felt drawn to explore the castle, to discover some quiet nook where she could be alone. BB-8 joined her.

Rey wandered along a passageway, finding a stone staircase that spiralled down into semidarkness. She descended. The last step took her into an underground corridor. BB-8 tittered, but she continued onward. The corridor led to a sealed door. Before she touched the lock, the door opened.

She entered what appeared to be a storeroom. Boxes were stacked under arches. Odd-sized containers packed the shelves. What tarps didn't cover was coated in a thick layer of dust.

In the middle of the room stood a small wooden table. On that table rested a small wooden box.

It caught Rey's interest like nothing else in the room. She went over to the box and opened it.

She heard breathing – more like ventilated rasping – and spun. The door she had entered had been replaced by a dark hallway. At the end, two silhouettes – one in a helmet and cloak, the other a young man seemingly not much older than her – dueled each other with laser blades. One red, the other blue. Lightsabers.

'Rey.'

She searched to see who had spoken her name. 'Hello?' No one responded. Not even BB-8. Where had he gone?

At the end of the hallway, a strange boy stared at her.

She hadn't taken more than a few steps towards him before everything around her whirled. Dizzy, she tumbled, sideways, into a wall that for some reason suddenly became a grassy field.

Into the grass stabbed a blade of crimson light. Then the skies clouded and darkened. Rain poured. The lightsaber was wrenched from the ground. It arced, like lightning in the storm.

The recipient of its swing was a man. She couldn't see his face. But she could hear his scream.

Drenched, she got up. Seven warriors, swathed in dark cloaks, advanced on her.

Rey tried to run. Tripping again, she glimpsed fire in the night. A temple in flames.

When she turned, the warriors were gone. In their place stood another cloaked figure and an R2 astromech unit. The figure touched a metal hand to the droid's silver dome.

Like the seven warriors, this scene also vanished.

In the blink of an eye, she was kneeling in a forest. Snow blanketed the ground and the limbs of trees. She'd never seen real snow before. Only sand.

She stood, shivering. Deep in the forest she heard the sounds of war. The ping of blasters. The sizzle of lightsabers. Death.

Someone spoke behind her. Calm, kind and eerily familiar. 'Stay here. I'll come back for you.'

She peered into the darkness between the trees. 'Where are you?'

'I'll come back, sweetheart. I promise.'

Rey did not want the owner of the voice to come back. She wanted the speaker to stay. 'I'm here! Right here! Where are you?'

As in her dreams, she heard no reply. She continued to dash through the forest, not giving up in her search.

A man in a metal mask, cloaked in black, strode out in front of her, the hilt of a lightsaber in his hand.

The cold stare of his mask stopped her dead in her tracks. Not one to scream, that's exactly what Rey did as she fell.

Snow didn't cushion her fall. The ground she hit was

made of stone. Aching, she sat up. She was once again in the subterranean hallway of the castle.

'There you are.' Maz stood in the corridor before the staircase.

Her head still spinning, Rey could barely get out the words. 'What . . . was *that*?'

Maz glanced at the doorway to the storeroom behind Rey. 'It called to you.'

Rey rose, shaky. 'I shouldn't have gone in there. I'm sorry.'

'Listen to me,' Maz said. 'This means something. Something very special—'

'I need to get back.' Rey took a deep breath, trying to steady herself.

'Yes, Han told me that,' Maz said, sounding compassionate. 'Whatever you've been waiting for – whomever – I can see it in your eyes, you've known it all along . . . they're not coming back. But there's someone who still *could*. With your help.'

After all Rey had been through – after seeing Finn walk away – her emotions were in turmoil. 'No.'

Maz held Rey's hand. 'That lightsaber was Luke's. And his father's before him. It reached out to you. The belonging you seek is not behind you. It is ahead. I am no Jedi, but I know the Force. It moves through and surrounds every living thing. Close your eyes. Feel it. The light. It's always been there. It will guide you.

'Take the saber.'

Rey recoiled. 'I'm never touching that thing again. I don't want any part of this!'

She dropped Maz's hand and ran. Up the stairs. Through the castle. Out into the forest. Never stopping.

Captain Phasma stood with a gaggle of generals and admirals on an elevated platform above the parade grounds of Starkiller Base. Assembled below them the military's best and brightest spread out in neat formations, all at attention. Rows of TIE fighters and walkers bordered the grounds, around which loomed treacherous snow-capped mountains.

Behind Phasma flapped what was perhaps the most impressive sight, the object on which everyone below was focused: a colossal flag of the First Order.

General Hux addressed the rally from the edge of the platform. 'This fierce machine which you have built, and upon which we stand, will bring a final end to the worthless Senate and the New Republic's cherished fleet.' His amplified voice echoed through the mountains. 'When this day is done, all the remaining systems will bow to the dictates of the First Order. All will remember this as the last day of the last Republic!'

It was quiet at first. Nothing but the icy breeze dusting snow back and forth across the parade grounds. Then there was an eruption. Out from the mountains shot a beam of light so intense many had to look away. Phasma's visor protected her from being blinded. She stared directly at the light. The sound came next, a shockwave that toppled many formations. Phasma stood tall, keeping her balance.

No one could see what happened then. The planet that was home to Starkiller Base was too distant from the intended target of the beam.

Outside the castle with Chewbacca, Han surveyed a section of Takodana's sky through a compact ponipin telescope. He'd heard many theories about the origin of the star that had recently blinked into existence. None made any sense. New stellar bodies didn't just brighten the sky all of a sudden.

Han's ponipin measured that the new star was also many, many light-years away, which under normal astronomical circumstances meant that it had actually blazed to life years before. Moreover, if the calculations proved correct, the stellar coordinates happened to be the same as those of the Hosnian system, where the capital of the New Republic was located.

Could the Hosnian system have gone nova? Could it – dare he even consider – have been *destroyed*? And if so, how had it happened so quickly?

'It was the Republic capital,' Finn said, approaching

Han and Chewie from behind. 'The First Order, they've gone and destroyed it.'

Han lowered the ponipin. His mind hatched worst-case scenarios. If Leia was in the capital—

'Where's Rey?' Finn's eyes roved the castle yard.

'I figured she was with you.'

Maz walked towards them. 'Rey is where she needs to be. You come with me. There's something you must see.'

Maz took Han, Chewbacca and Finn back into the castle, then down a flight of stairs, into a storeroom packed with crates. She went over to a small table on which rested an opened box. She reached into the box and took out a cylinder of a quarter arm's length.

Han knew what it was because he had seen it in action. He'd even used it himself. It was the hilt of Luke Skywalker's lightsaber.

'Where'd you get that?' he demanded.

Maz admired the hilt in her spindly fingers. 'Long story. A good one – for later.' To everyone's surprise, she looked at Finn next. 'Your friend is in grave danger,' she said. 'Take this – and find Rey.'

She held out the hilt to Finn. He took it.

A detonation shook them all. Bits of the ceiling rained down. The rumbling continued in other areas. It wasn't a firefight that had gotten out of control or an old grenade losing its cap. The castle was under attack.

'Those beasts. They're here,' Maz said.

CHAPTER
14

REY finally stopped running, deep in the forest. She didn't know why she had been running for so long; she had just felt the need. Now all she felt was exhaustion.

Announcing himself with a beep, BB-8 rolled towards her. She blinked. Was she seeing things again? Had he really followed her all that way?

The astromech unit chirped a question of his own. He wanted to know where she intended they go. *They?* Just because the two of them had travelled together in the past, it didn't mean they would do so in the future. Finn had reminded her of that.

But despite her pleas, the little droid refused to leave her. He would go wherever she went, to Jakku and back again if that's what she wanted.

'No. You have to go back to them,' she said. 'You're important. Much more than I am. They'll help you fulfill your mission, more than I ever could.'

The skies rumbled. Through a break in the treetops,

she glimpsed a squadron of warships descending in the direction of Maz's castle. An insignia of a saw-toothed circle inside a red square was emblazoned on all the craft.

The First Order had found them.

Rey sprinted towards the castle. She couldn't leave Han Solo or Chewbacca to a First Order firing squad. Solo had offered her a job as part of his crew. She would show him that he was right to place trust in her loyalty.

Emerging atop a hill overlooking the castle, she saw she was too late. TIE fighters flew patterns around the fortress, levelling it with laser cannons. Stormtroopers leapt out of transports to secure what remained and shoot what still moved.

Rey went around the forest's edge to see if she could sneak into the castle from the rear. A shuttle coming in to land prevented that. Out from its hatch disembarked a cloaked figure in a metal mask.

The same figure she had seen in her vision under the castle.

Blaster shots rang out, setting the trees on fire around her. A stormtrooper squad had seen her. She ducked behind a tree, returning fire with her pistol – or she had hoped to. It wasn't until she flipped the safety that something other than a *click-click* issued from the blaster. Her first real round of shots did its job, nailing two troopers and forcing the squad to fall back.

Rey also fell back into the brush for more cover.

'Keep going, stay out of sight,' she said to a concerned BB-8. 'I'll fight 'em off.'

The droid complied with her command this time and sped ahead into the woods. Rey continued at a slower pace, blaster ready.

Without warning or sound, the man in the mask strode out from the darkness of the forest. How he had managed to get in front of her, she could hardly guess. But she didn't have to guess his purpose. He ignited the long red blade of his lightsaber. Perpendicular to its hilt, two licks of laser-flame formed a fiery guard that would pose a danger to the wielder's hand, unless the wielder had complete mastery of the weapon.

Rey fired her blaster.

His lightsaber flew up and batted away every shot she took.

She kept pulling the trigger. There was nothing else she could do. He deflected her bolts, then reached out with his palm.

All her limbs cramped. She was incapable of physical movement. Not her legs, not her arms, not her fingers. It was even hard to breathe.

The man stalked towards her. His voice, filtered through the mask, mocked her. 'You would *kill* me, knowing nothing about me?'

Rey's tongue remained mobile. 'Why wouldn't I kill you? I know about the First Order.'

He circled her. 'So afraid, yet I am the one who should be scared. You shot first. You speak of the Order as if it were barbaric. Yet, it is I who was forced to defend myself against you.'

He stepped close to her, raising his blade to cast its fiery light on her flesh. 'Something. There is something.' He stared at her through his visor. *'Who are you?'*

Though her tongue and lips could move, Rey didn't let them. She wouldn't tell him anything.

The masked man deactivated his lightsaber and hung it on his belt. His gloved hand grazed her temple and cheeks. She shifted her eyes so she wouldn't have to look at him.

She could still feel him. His presence tickled her mind. Phantom tendrils slithered through her thoughts. Memories of her youth flashed before her like data on a readout.

He sounded disappointed. 'Is it true, then? You're nothing special after all? You're just a Jakku scavenger?'

Rey pursed her lips. His tendrils continued to worm around her mind – beginning to burrow deeper, as if their tips were scalpels. The more she tried to push back, the sharper the tendrils became.

They wrapped themselves around an image of Finn she held in her mind's eye. 'You've met the traitor who served under me. You've even begun to care for him.'

She struggled, trying to think of anything, anyone

else. Then she realised that gave him the access he wanted. 'You've seen it – the map!'

Her mind thrashed as his phantom tendrils dug into her memories like claws. Mercifully, she blanked into unconsciousness.

When they got above ground, Maz's order to Finn was simple. 'Find the girl and the droid.'

Finn glanced at the rubble that surrounded them. He'd lost his blaster in their escape from the castle. 'I need a weapon.'

Maz seized his wrist. 'You have one.'

He activated the blade. It hummed in his hand, bearing little weight. When he swished it through the air, it felt like an extension of his arm. A deadly extension.

Its bright blue beam also alerted an enemy squad. Stormtroopers began blasting at them.

Han and Chewbacca dove for cover and shot back. Three stormtroopers emerged behind them, aiming at the unaware duo. Finn did the only thing he could think of to save the pair. He rushed the troopers.

The troopers were as startled as Finn when he sliced through armour, bone and flesh. Two he cut down immediately. The third trooper dropped his rifle and brandished a melee weapon of his own, a riot control baton that crackled with blue electricity. Finn swung at him, but the trooper ducked and shoved Finn backward, off his feet. The trooper had raised his baton to finish Finn when a blaster bolt finished the trooper instead.

The shooter was none other than Han Solo. The old smuggler and the Wookiee ran over to Finn.

'You OK?' Han asked, giving him a hand up.

Finn picked up his lightsaber, which had retracted when he'd fallen. 'I'm OK, yeah. Thanks.'

How much longer he'd stay OK was the real question. Stormtrooper reinforcements arrived to circle them, outnumbering them more than three to one. 'Drop the weapons – now!' the trooper shouted.

Han and Chewbacca did as ordered. Finn let go of his lightsaber reluctantly. A trooper stepped forward and retrieved it.

His two companions murmured and growled about what to do next. There wasn't anything to be done when a second squad approached. They were all captives of the First Order and would probably never see the stars again.

Finn took a final look at the sky to see stars streaking down at him.

Not stars – X-wings.

A squadron of them swooped over the lake, cannons firing at any First Order ships that dared engage. Most of the TIEs were parked around the remains of the castle, not expecting a surprise attack. The TIE fighters became what they'd turned the castle into – smoking ruins.

'It's the Resistance!' Han cheered.

Everyone, captors and captives alike, scrambled for cover. White armour marked easy targets for the X-wings. Stormtroopers fell in large numbers.

Finn went for a dropped rifle, then decided against it. He wanted the weapon Maz had given him. He recovered the lightsaber from a fallen stormtrooper.

The lead X-wing, black with orange racing stripes, veered around to strafe the remaining stormtroopers and TIEs. 'That's one heckuva pilot,' Finn said to himself.

Finn glimpsed a figure marching out of the forest towards a waiting shuttle. He wore a cloak and mask, and seemed unconcerned about the stormtroopers dying around him.

Kylo Ren.

He carried in his arms a pale young woman.

'Rey!'

Finn dashed towards the shuttle. Enemy fire laced all around him. 'No, no, no . . . Rey – *Rey!*'

His shouts were lost in the boom of liftoff. The First Order shuttle and a few other undamaged craft rocketed towards the atmosphere.

Finn was fighting tears when he returned to the castle and found Han. 'He took her,' Finn said. 'Did you see that? She's gone. Rey's gone!'

Han pushed past Finn. 'Get out of my way.'

Finn halted, stunned. A few metres away, he heard

Maz speaking softly to BB-8. 'Yes, they have Rey now,' she said. The droid beeped. 'I know. But we can't give up hope. Share what you have with your people. They need you.'

The droid rolled off obediently. Maz walked over to Finn. 'Looks like I've got some cleaning up to do, hmmm?' She stared at him through her goggles and smiled. 'Oh. Wow.'

'What?' Finn asked.

'I see something else now,' she said. 'Now I see the eyes of a warrior.'

His son had played a part in the attack. *Their* son.

His heart on the verge of breaking, Han stood amid the wreckage of battle and looked upon a woman he hadn't seen in a long time. She disembarked from the Resistance transport that had landed near the castle. The plain jumpsuit she had on was a far cry from the royal robes she'd worn when he'd first laid eyes on her, in a Death Star corridor, decades before. Her brown hair had turned grey, and while it was still braided, it lacked the finesse of her youth.

She walked towards Han, her regal posture undiminished. Her protocol droid, golden once, now a blemished bronze except for one transplanted red arm, bumbled beside her. His official designation was C-3PO, though Han had plenty of other names for him. History had accorded the woman many names and titles, from princess of Alderaan to leader of the Resistance, but to Han she was simply Leia. His wife.

BB-8 rolled away with C-3PO for a droid debriefing. Han had learned that it was C-3PO who had discovered their location on Takodana. An ordinary GA servant droid in Maz's castle was part of a Resistance spy network and had transmitted to C-3PO that BB-8 was there. Which meant Han owed his life to old Goldenrod, though he'd never admit it.

Once the droids were gone, husband and wife shared a moment together, alone.

'You changed your hair,' Han said.

She raised an eye at his outfit. 'Same jacket.'

'No. New jacket.'

Their peace was short-lived. Striding towards them, Chewbacca burst out with an elated roar and enveloped Leia in his arms. His grunts and *wroofs* made her smile. Satisfied, the Wookiee boarded the transport.

The two followed the Wookiee's example and embraced. Han could hardly remember the last time he'd held Leia so near. He missed her. And he regretted having to ruin the moment with news of their son.

'I saw him,' Han said. 'He was here.'

Leia closed her eyes but did not seem surprised, as if she had already known.

CHAPTER
15

NAVIGATING D'Qar's asteroid belt felt like a pleasant pastime after the perils Poe had faced on Jakku. He steered his X-wing around the orbiting rocks with ease, then descended through the verdant planet's atmosphere and forest canopy to touch down before Resistance headquarters. The base was as he had left it before striking out on his mission. Creeper vines weaved patterns around duracrete buildings and bunkers, camouflaging them from view overhead. Unlike the shifting sands of Jakku, the ground remained firm under Poe's feet.

It was good to be home.

An overenthusiastic BB-8 bulleted across the landing area and deluged him with beeps. Poe turned his head to see the stormtrooper he had named Finn approaching.

'Poe, Poe Dameron,' Finn said with a big grin, 'you're alive!'

'So are you,' Poe observed, returning the smile.

'What happened?'

'I regained consciousness after you ejected from the TIE and managed to avoid a complete crash – but not a miserable trek through the desert. If a scavenger hadn't given me a ride and helped me off Jakku, I'd be buried in a sand dune. But that's nothing compared to what you've done. I heard you completed my mission, and best of all, you saved my jacket.'

Finn started to pull it off. 'Sorry – here.'

Poe motioned him to stop. 'Keep it. It suits you. I've got a new one.' He grinned. The galaxy sure worked in mysterious ways. Both of them had been trained to be enemies, yet above all odds, there they were as friends. 'You're a good man, Finn. The Resistance needs the help of more like you.'

'Poe, I need your help.'

When Poe heard the specific nature of Finn's request, he took the former stormtrooper into the base to meet the one person who *could* help.

'General, sorry to interrupt, but this is Finn and he needs to talk to you.'

General Leia Organa excused herself from a conference with senior command staff and turned to Poe and his companion. 'And I need to talk to him,' she said. 'That was incredibly brave, what you did.'

'Thank you, ma'am,' Finn said, 'but I'm here to talk

about a friend of mine who was taken prisoner during the clash on Takodana.'

She sighed. 'Han told me about the girl. I'm sorry.'

'Finn's familiar with the weapon that destroyed the Hosnian system,' Poe said. 'He worked on the planet where it was built.'

Leia took Finn's hand. 'We're desperate for anything you can tell us.'

'It's located on the world that serves as the First Order's main base,' Finn said. 'I'm sure that's where they've taken my friend. I need to get there, fast.'

'The girl. What's her name?' Leia asked.

'Rey,' Finn said softly.

Rey woke to find herself bound to an interrogation bench, tilted almost to a standing position. The interrogator himself lurked nearby, watching her through his metal mask.

'Where am I?' she asked him.

'You're my guest,' he said, not the least bit invitingly.

He gestured. Her shackles popped loose. She massaged the areas where her arms had been compressed. 'Where are the others? The ones who were fighting with me?'

He snorted. 'You mean the traitors, murderers and thieves you call friends? You will be relieved to hear that I have no idea.'

Relief was the last emotion Rey could've felt. How

could she believe anything he said? She seethed with anger at him, desperate to tear the man's mask off and hammer it into his skull. He regarded her with the same cold metallic expression. 'You still want to kill me.'

'That happens when you're being hunted by a creature in a mask.'

He held her stare, and then his gloved hands touched the sides of his mask and took it off.

He had a young man's face, with an old man's eyes. His lips and dark hair stood out against the pale complexion of one who shirked the sun. He looked like a student who took no joy in his studies. One who perceived only the great problems of the galaxy and not its simple pleasures.

'Tell me about the droid,' he said.

'It's a BB unit with a selenium drive and a thermal hyperscan vindicator, internal self-correcting gyroscopic propulsion system, optics corrected to—'

His eyes pinched. 'The map. It's what I need.'

She kept her mouth shut and tried to forget what she had seen. Yet the harder she tried to forget, the more she saw the map in her mind. This was one of his tricks, she realised. She had to start thinking of something else.

'I can take whatever I want,' he said to her.

'Then you don't need me to tell you anything.'

'True,' he said. His fingers stroked her face.

Released from her restraints, she could have pushed

him away, which was probably what he wanted. But that would have broken her concentration. And she needed all of it to block him from probing deeper.

She built her barrier out of the very emotion that had sustained her since ever she could remember.

'You've been so lonely. So afraid to leave.' His tendrils crept around her memories, her dreams. 'At night, desperate to sleep, you imagine an ocean. I can see it. I can see the island.'

Focusing on her loneliness, recalling the sadness that plagued her life, brought tears to Rey's eyes. They streamed down her face, droplets that would have been precious on Jakku.

'And Han Solo,' he said. 'He feels like the father you never had.'

His tone softened, as if he cared. 'Let it go. He would disappoint you.'

Rey knew this was a ploy. The man did not care about anything other than himself and his goals. 'Get . . . out . . . of my . . . head!' she fumed.

'Rey,' he said, pulling out her name from the echoes of her thoughts, 'you've seen the map. It's in there. And I'm going to take it. Don't be afraid.'

Fear. That's not what she felt. She wasn't afraid of him. She knew what he could do and was trying to fight him. No. He was talking about himself. What *he* felt. His weakness. Fear was the portal into *his* mind.

She turned his tendrils back at him. His feelings and memories were easy to read. His mind was a turbulent ocean of fear. 'You, you're afraid. That you will never be as strong as—' She hesitated. An image of another man in a black cloak and mask dominated the maelstrom. A silhouette she had seen in the vision below Maz's castle. He had a name. 'Darth Vader.'

The gloved hand jerked away from her face. Her interrogator staggered, as if hammered by an invisible blow.

He waved and the shackles clamped her wrists, much tighter this time. The pain they inflicted did not diminish her gratification at watching him stumble out of the cell, humbled and defeated.

Han sat in the situation room with the senior Resistance commanders. He drummed his fingers, waiting for C-3PO to remove an odd object from BB-8. Han had already told everyone that the map was incomplete, but Leia insisted that she and her staff have a look for themselves.

Having carefully removed the object, C-3PO slipped it into a round table in the centre of the room. Above the table, the star map materialised at a larger magnification than Han had first seen in the *Falcon*. Leia and her people studied the map while Han studied their faces. No one seemed happy about what they saw.

C-3PO voiced their disappointment. 'General, unfortunately this map contains insufficient data from which to match any system in our records.'

'Told you,' Han couldn't help but add.

Leia shook her head. 'What a fool I was to think we could just find Luke and bring him back.'

Han softened, seeing his wife so distressed. 'Leia—'

'Don't do that,' she snapped.

'Do what?'

'Be nice to me.' She marched out of the room.

Han went after her. 'Hey, I'm here to help.'

She kept walking down the corridor. 'When did that ever *help*? And don't say the Death Star.'

He got in front of her. 'Will you just stop and listen to me for a minute? Please?'

She huffed. She still had the patience of a princess, which was little. But she stopped and looked up at him. 'I'm listening, Han.'

Han didn't sugarcoat his words. She was immune to such charms. So he went straight to the root of the conflict – their son. 'I didn't plan on coming here. I know whenever you look at me, you're reminded of him. So I stayed away.'

'That's what you think? That I don't want to be reminded of him? That I want to forget him?' She shook her head. 'I want him back.'

'He's gone, Leia. He was always drawn to the dark

side. There was nothing we could have done to stop it, no matter how hard we tried. There was too much . . . Vader in him.'

'That's why I wanted him to train with Luke,' Leia said. 'I just never should have sent him away. That's when I lost him. Lost you both.'

'We both had to deal with it in our own way,' Han said. 'I went back to the only thing I was ever good at.'

'We both did,' Leia said sadly.

'We've lost our son forever.'

'No,' Leia said. 'It was Snoke.'

'Snoke?'

'He knew our child would be strong with the Force,' Leia said. 'That he was born with equal potential for good or evil.'

'You knew this from the beginning? Why didn't you tell me?' Han asked.

Leia said nothing in her defense. Han didn't push. 'So Snoke was watching our son.'

'Always. From the shadows,' Leia explained. 'Even before I realised what was happening, he was manipulating everything, pulling our son towards the dark side.'

Han sighed. There were many days he wished he'd never heard about such things. The Force perplexed him. He would've given everything for his son to be ordinary - like him. It was easier to make the Kessel Run in eleven parsecs than to turn someone back from the dark side.

'But nothing's impossible, Han. I have this feeling if anyone can save him, it's you.'

'*Me?*' Han frowned. 'No. If Luke couldn't reach him, with all his skills and training, how can I?'

'Luke is a Jedi. But you're his father. There's still light in him, I know it.'

CHAPTER
16

KYLO REN knelt before his shadowy master in the command chamber of Starkiller Base and reported his failure.

'This scavenger, this *girl*, resisted you?' Supreme Leader Snoke's hologram, large and imposing on the dais, glared down at Ren.

'That's all she is, yes. A scavenger from Jakku. Completely untrained, but strong with the Force. Stronger than she knows,' Ren said, rising.

'You have compassion for her.'

'*Compassion?* For an enemy of the Order? No, never,' Ren insisted.

'It isn't her strength that is making you fail. It's your weakness,' Snoke said. 'Where is the droid?'

The echo of boots on the chamber floor preceded the voice of General Hux. 'Ren believed it was no longer of value to us. He believed that he could obtain everything that was necessary from the girl. As a result, it is likely that the droid has been returned to the hands of the enemy.'

Ren felt his master's anger, though Snoke's voice

betrayed none of it. 'Have we located the main Resistance base?'

The general halted before the dais and bowed. 'We were able to track their reconnaissance ship back to the Ileenium system. We are coordinating with our own spy vessels to lock down the specific location of their base.'

'We do not need it. Prepare the weapon. Destroy their system,' the Supreme Leader said.

Hux lost his composure. 'The *system*? Supreme Leader, we will have the location of the base within a matter of hours and—'

'We cannot wait. The more time we give them, the more likely the chance that they will find Skywalker and convince him to return to challenge our power.'

Ren summoned confidence. 'Supreme Leader, I can get the map from the girl, and that will be the end of it. I just need your guidance.'

The Supreme Leader's hologram roiled like storm clouds at dusk. 'And you promised me when it came to destroying the Resistance, you wouldn't fail me.'

Ren trembled, his confidence snuffed out.

'General, prepare the weapon.'

'Yes, Supreme Leader.' Hux saluted and marched out of the command room.

'Kylo Ren,' the Supreme Leader said, 'it appears that a reminder is in order. I must show you the power of the dark side. Bring the girl to me.'

Finn peered at a three-dimensional representation of the icy world on which he'd trained. Around him in the vine-covered situation room stood the highest-ranking commanders of the Resistance. Among those whom Finn recognised were Admiral Statura, General Organa and Admiral Ackbar, the legendary Mon Calamari commander of the Rebel Alliance's historic victory at Endor. All grim and grave, they examined the planetary map that projected from a central circular table.

Poe Dameron and Captain Snap Wexley, a dark-haired pilot, stepped forth to inform the staff of what Finn had told them. The planet, only known to Finn as Starkiller Base, contained a weapon that lived up to the name. Harnessing the planetary core as a dynamo and using the system's sun as a lens, the Starkiller weapon could shoot a blast of energy – dark energy, to be precise – through hyperspace at other stars or planets. The strike would trigger the target's core to implode into the stellar dust from which it was formed.

'It's another Death Star,' said a bearded veteran with long white hair, referring to the Empire's planet-killing battle station from three decades before.

'I wish that were the case, Major Ematt.' Poe loaded up another spherical hologram. 'This was the Death Star.' Metal, rather than snowy forests and frozen mountains, covered the orb, and a crater that was its superlaser focusing lens carved out its northern hemisphere. The Death Star was but a small moon next to the hologram of the icy planet. 'This is Starkiller Base.'

Finn spoke up. 'General Hux told us it's the most powerful weapon ever built. He said that it can reach halfway across the galaxy.'

The officers' attentive silence devolved into nervous chatter. An irritated Han Solo broke in. 'I don't care how big it is. How do we blow it up?'

Silence returned.

Though slim and short in stature, Admiral Statura instantly had all eyes fixed on him when he stepped forward. 'The weapon would be at its most vulnerable when it is fully loaded. If the containment field oscillator were somehow destroyed, it would release the accumulated energy not in a line of fire, but throughout the planetary core. If it did not result in the complete destruction of the base, at the very least it would permanently cripple the weapon.'

Admiral Ackbar shook his salmon-coloured head. His guttural voice sounded as if he were speaking underwater, which was the native habitat of his species. 'None of this is possible. The instant we move forces out of hiding, the First Order will realise we know the location of the weapon. They will mobilise their own ships to protect it. Their fleet is too large for us to fight our way through.'

General Organa showed everyone the datapad she had been reading during the briefing. 'According to this, we don't have time to study the situation. They're loading the weapon again. I think we can all take a good guess as to what their next target will be.'

Finn's heart fell. His new friends stood no chance against the Starkiller. He almost suggested they should run – but to where?

Poe blunted the flagging spirits by proposing an idea. 'They may raise their shields, but if we can find a way past them, we can and will hit that oscillator with everything we've got.'

'Any plan is pointless as long as their shields are in place,' Ackbar countered.

Han wasn't dismayed. 'OK, so first we disable the shields. Kid, you worked there. What'cha got?'

He was looking at Finn. In a matter of seconds, so was everyone in the room. They were relying on him. So was someone else. Someone he might be able to save if he could sneak onto Starkiller Base.

'I can shut down their shields. I know where their relevant controls are located,' Finn said. 'But I need to be there. On the planet, with access to the location.'

'I'll get you there,' Han said, without hesitation.

General Organa turned to her husband. 'Han, how?'

Han gave her the same crooked grin Finn had seen him give Rey. 'If I told you, you wouldn't like it.'

With the plan set, everyone left to make preparations. For the first time since he'd deserted the First Order, Finn felt that his training would be of good use.

Han yelled at the techs working on the *Falcon* to scram and began doing the needed maintenance himself. Mostly, that involved giving orders. 'Chewie, check the horizontal booster. Finn, careful with those dentons – they're explosives.'

Finn looked down in worry at the crate he was hauling. 'They are? Why didn't you tell me?'

'Didn't want to make you nervous,' Han said. 'When you've finished loading those, go talk to some of those X-wing techs and see if you can scare us up a backup thermal regulator.'

A voice turned Han away from the *Falcon*. 'No matter how much we fought, I always hated watching you leave,' Leia said, walking towards him.

'That's why I left,' he said with a smirk. 'To make you miss me.'

Leia chuckled. 'Well, thank you for that, anyway.'

'Some things never change,' he said.

'Yep. You still drive me crazy.'

He touched her shoulders and became serious. 'Leia, there's something I've been wanting to say to you for a long time.'

She reached up and touched her finger to his lips. 'Tell me when you get back.'

He embraced his wife.

'If you see our son, bring him home,' she said.

Han held Leia tight, determined to do just as she said.

CHAPTER
17

REY lay restrained on the interrogation bench. But she didn't feel like a prisoner. Something had happened when she had pushed back against her captor's mind. She'd felt a release, as if a pair of shackles had shattered. Shackles that held not her wrists but her . . . *self*?

She didn't fully understand. There would be time for further introspection if she got out of here. As of then, it didn't look like it was going to happen. The restraints clamping her to the bench were not going to snap, no matter how hard she pushed. And even if she did break out, she'd still have to deal with the stormtrooper inside her cell, guarding her door.

But maybe there was another way out. She had pushed back at her captor through sheer will, the force of her mind. Maybe with a little luck she could call on that strength again.

'You,' she said to the trooper.

The trooper looked at her, his expression unreadable

behind his helmet. That made what she was about to try easier. She was not distracted by his individuality. She saw only a faceless drone of the First Order. And one thing drones did was obey commands.

'You will remove these restraints,' she told the guard. 'And you will leave the cell, with the door open, and retire to your living quarters.'

The trooper continued to stare at her. He must've thought her crazy to believe that he'd listen to her. Maybe she was.

Rey tried again. Directing the will of her mind past his helmet, into his mind, as she had with her interrogator.

She repeated her command, enunciating each word in her speech and in her mind so it would echo in his.

The trooper walked towards her, his blaster rifle at the ready. 'I will remove these restraints. And leave this cell, with the door open, and retire to my living quarters. I will speak of this encounter to no one.'

He did as commanded, liberating her from the shackles. She continued to recline on the bench, stunned that her prompt had actually worked.

The trooper turned and went for the door, still carrying his rifle.

'And you will drop your weapon,' she said.

There was no hesitation. 'I will drop my weapon,' he said. He set it on the floor, opened the cell door and headed out, presumably to his living quarters.

She remained on the bench. The cell door was open. The rifle was on the ground. The stormtrooper was gone.

When he didn't come back, Rey knew she wasn't crazy. She also knew that what she'd just done had nothing to do with luck.

Finn should have been resting on the *Falcon*'s trip through hyperspace, but his mind wouldn't switch off. He tried playing holochess, losing twice to the computer in record time. Nothing would distract him. Nothing would calm his mind. He recalled his visions of glory on the First Order transport to Jakku. His exuberance.

He thought of Slip.

Finn could've easily shared FN-2003's fate. And if he had, what would the state of the galaxy be now? Would BB-8 have made it to D'Qar? Would Poe have been another of the First Order's victims? Would Rey still be salvaging wrecks, safe from capture?

Finn hadn't been taught to contemplate such questions. He'd been trained to shoot and fight. He knew he'd have to rely on those skills when they got to Starkiller Base – *if* they got there. He still had no clue how the *Falcon* would slip through the planetary shields in the first place.

Quitting the lounge, Finn bothered Han and Chewie in the cockpit. 'How are we getting in?'

Han continued to work his controls. 'No planetary

defense system can be sustained at a constant rate. It would take too much power. The shields fluctuate at a predetermined rate. Keeps anything travelling less than lightspeed from getting through.'

'But how are we getting in? Without being cut in half by the oscillating shield?' Finn asked.

'Easy. We won't be going slower than lightspeed.'

'We're gonna make our landing approach at lightspeed? Nobody's ever done that!'

Chewbacca growled something that made Han grin. 'We're coming up on the system. I'd sit down if I were you,' Han said to Finn. 'Chewie, get ready.'

Finn dropped into a seat and buckled himself in. Han and Chewbacca watched the scroll of data on multiple monitors. 'And . . .' Han paused. *'Now!'*

The two pilots worked in tandem, pulling levers, pushing buttons, turning dials. When they came out of lightspeed, Finn blinked and saw he was still alive. They'd beaten the odds. Scanners showed they had jumped inside the shield of Starkiller Base.

But at the speed they were going, Finn wondered how many blinks he had left. They were on a swift trajectory to crash into the planet's surface.

'I am pulling up!' Han shouted at his copilot. 'Any higher, they'll see us!'

The two managed to level the *Falcon* before it crashed, but they did not avert a rough landing. Splintering the treetops of a large swath of forest, the *Millennium Falcon* finally skidded to a halt in a snowfield.

Kylo Ren marched down a rock-cut corridor on Starkiller Base. The buildup of energies in the planetary core mirrored the tempest brewing inside him. The girl, he'd been informed, had somehow broken out of her cell.

He didn't ask many questions of the officer who had reported the escape, or the trooper who had guarded her. He went to see for himself.

The cell was empty.

He activated his lightsaber. Screaming and slashing, he sawed apart the interrogation bench, then went to work on the walls.

The furnace of his heart had a source of its own dark energy. It was called fury.

CHAPTER
18

HAN trudged through the snowy forest with Chewbacca and Finn. His legs ached, and the freezing wind was fierce when it gusted through the trees. He was getting too old for this sort of thing.

Han also didn't like leaving the *Millennium Falcon* half-buried in a snowdrift. He'd given her a good-luck tap when he'd disembarked. He didn't know what he'd do if he lost her again. The fact that he had found her against the greatest of odds – 19,077,000 to 1, C-3PO had told him – gave Han hope that maybe, at the end, everything would turn out all right.

Finn indicated a break in the forest ahead. 'There's a flood tunnel over that ridge. We can get in that way.'

It all felt a little too easy to Han. 'You sure the tunnel isn't safety screened?' he asked. 'We can cut through ordinary stuff, but—'

'There's no screen at all. A screen would defeat the tunnel's purpose.'

Han looked at the kid. 'You said you were stationed here. You never told us your specialty.'

'Sanitation,' Finn said.

'*Sanitation?* How do you know how to take down the shields?'

'I don't know how to take down the shields, Han,' Finn said matter-of-factly. 'I'm here to get Rey.'

Chewbacca grumbled. Han spun on Finn. 'Anything else you've overlooked? Anything else you've forgotten to tell us? People are counting on us. *The galaxy* is counting on us!'

'Solo, we got here, didn't we? We'll figure it out.'

'Yeah, how?' Because Han was all out of ideas.

Finn flashed a crooked grin of his own. 'We'll use the Force.'

'I haven't got time to explain it to you, kid, but that's *not* how the Force works.'

He couldn't have explained it if he *did* have time. He didn't tell Finn that.

Rey hurried down passageway after passageway, carrying her former guard's blaster rifle. Metal plated some walls while others showed jagged rock, offering nooks and crannies to duck into when she sensed anyone approaching.

She arrived at a narrow walkway that had been built along a wall. On its open side, the walkway lacked a railing to prevent plunges down a deep chasm. But beyond the walkway, Rey saw a means of flight out of here. TIE fighters were docked in a hangar.

Stormtroopers guarded the doorway. Chatting among themselves, they hadn't noticed her. Neither had the stormtroopers she heard approaching. But if she didn't do something soon, one or both patrols would discover her.

Rey strapped the rifle over her shoulder and dropped over the side of the walkway.

She didn't fall into the chasm. She hung. Gripping the edge of the walkway with her fingers and bracing her feet against the wall. She'd had practise doing this sort of thing. Salvaging on Jakku had necessitated many similar precarious climbs. The important thing was never to look down.

Surveying the area under the walkway, Rey glimpsed a hatch on the far wall.

She lifted one hand off the edge and moved it a half metre before setting it down, testing the grip. She did the same with a foot, finding shelves in the stone that held. Continuing this process, Rey crept along the walkway. Balance was vital. She never looked down.

Within reach of her destination, she elbowed the access panel. The hatch opened. She crawled through, into a maintenance bay.

A repair droid trundled towards her, then continued

past to perform some preprogrammed function. Rey hastened across the bay, not trusting that another droid would be so ignorant.

Finn knew the layout of the dark flood tunnels like he knew how to clean his rifle. He could travel through the maze with a blast shield over his eyes and still get where he wanted to be.

He guided Han and Chewbacca through the sludge to an unmarked portal in the sewers. It was intended only for emergency transport of cleaning supplies, but those in the sanitation crew often used it as a quick entrance point into the base.

Finn tapped a code and the portal opened.

'The less time spent here, the better luck we're going to have,' Han advised.

'Yeah, I know,' Finn said.

He took them through the corridors that he recalled were less frequently patrolled. He chose well, because they encountered no one.

Their first glimpse of real activity in the base gave Finn pause. Another stormtrooper headed in their direction, wearing a black cape and chrome armour that had been polished clean since the raid on Jakku.

It was his old commander, Captain Phasma.

Finn's worry vanished when he realised she would be the key to disabling the shields. He and Han ducked back while Chewbacca stepped out, disarmed her and pulled her around the corner.

Finn raised his weapon at her helmet. 'Captain Phasma, remember me? Still want to inspect my blaster?'

Phasma struggled in the Wookiee's grip. 'Yes, I remember you, Eff-Enn-Two-One-Eight-Seven.'

'Not anymore. My name is Finn. A real name for a real person. And I'm in charge now.'

With the Wookiee clutching her arm and Han's pistol joining Finn's to point at her, Phasma had no choice but to go with them into the shield control room.

No one was there. Since the shields ran on automatic systems, techs visited only to troubleshoot any issues. Architects hadn't even considered potential intrusion. Who in their right mind would sneak so deep into the First Order's main military base?

Finn preferred not to be in his right mind when it came to the dictates of the First Order. It was his one true advantage. Its officers were so blinded by their own training regimen, they could not predict what someone like him – an anomaly – would do next.

He planted Phasma at a console and ordered her to initiate the deactivation. When she refused, he pressed his blaster harder against her helmet. 'Do it.'

She did. A few keystrokes were all it took to bypass the automatic systems and start the sequence to shut down the shields.

Finn watched the shield generator levels decline. 'Solo, if I remember correctly what they told us about the shield system, we don't have a lot of time to find Rey.'

'Don't worry, kid. We won't leave here without her.' Han kept his blaster trained on Phasma. 'But what do we do about her? Is there a garbage chute or trash compactor nearby?'

'Yeah, there is.'

When the shields were fully powered down and the consoles had been blasted beyond repair, they dumped Phasma down a chute into the base's sewage. Finn felt sorry only for her armour.

CHAPTER
19

'BLACK LEADER.' The voice crackled over Poe's X-wing hypercomm. 'Go to sublight. Attack, repeat, attack on your call.'

Poe smiled. He and the two squadrons under his command, Red and Blue, had been travelling through hyperspace near Starkiller Base, awaiting orders from Resistance headquarters. He'd started to worry that word would never come. But it did, meaning Finn's team had accomplished their mission. The shields were down.

'Roger, Base,' he commed back. He sent a command to BB-8 in the astromech socket. 'Red Squad, Blue Squad, follow my lead.'

'Copy that, Black Leader.' Captain Wexley's voice came through loud and clear.

The other pilots also chimed in to confirm, including Nien Nunb, the celebrated Sullustan who'd flown the *Millennium Falcon* with Lando Calrissian at Endor, and Jess Pava in Blue Three, a young spitfire whose prowess in an X-wing exceeded that of many more experienced fighter jockeys.

The pilots had bragged that the forthcoming battle would be one for the history books, like Yavin and Endor. Poe didn't join in that talk. History could take care of itself. His job was to ensure they fulfilled their objective and to keep enough of them alive to brag.

All the lifts heading up to the hangar required security passcodes. Rey didn't want to risk entering a false code and alerting the base to her location. She waited to see if she might be able to catch a ride with any of the droids, but none of them seemed to have duties above.

She was stuck.

The ceiling rumbled. Through a ventilation grate she saw TIE fighters launch out of the hangar. Maybe they were doing a flight exercise, or maybe there was an attack on the base. Whatever the cause, her means of escape had rocketed away. She had to look for another way out.

Rey pried open a floor grate and crawled down a ventilation shaft. She heard voices in the corridor above. The shaft was not fully covered on its path up the corridor's wall. She had to shimmy up quickly not to be noticed.

But she was noticed. By Han Solo of all people. He stood in the corridor and grinned at her. Chewbacca was there, too, as was someone else she never thought she'd see again.

Rey and Finn gave each other the biggest of hugs. 'Are you all right? What happened?' Finn asked. 'Did he hurt you?'

'Never mind me, what are you doing here?'

Finn tried to play it cool. 'We came back for you.'

Chewbacca ruffed, which told Rey what she had thought and hoped.

Finn glanced at the Wookiee. 'What did he say?'

'That it was your idea,' Rey said.

Han stepped in before the reunion turned too emotional. 'We'll have a party later. I'll bring the cake. Right now, let's get outta here.'

Rey couldn't agree with him more. But she'd hold Han to his promise when all was said and done. In her nineteen years, she had never tasted cake.

Poe triggered his X-wing lasers at the TIE fighters that launched from the enemy base. 'Cover for each other!' he commed to his squadrons. 'There's a lot of them, but that just means more targets. Don't let these thugs scare you!'

'Blue Three, you got one on your tail,' Snap Wexley barked over the comm. 'Pull up and give us a view!'

'Copy that,' answered Jess. Her X-wing made an

abrupt ascent, revealing the TIE that was in pursuit. Poe blasted it into parts.

'I owe you one,' Jess said.

'Yeah, you owe me another attack run,' Poe replied. 'Try to stay close, all teams – follow me in!'

The TIEs swarmed them in greater numbers, breaking the X-wings' formations. A few of his squadron mates stuck with Poe and began a bombing run over the hexagonal facility that housed the Starkiller oscillator. They dropped everything they could on the structure, enough to pulverise a small city. Yet when Poe looked back, the facility was still standing, showing only minimal damage.

'We're not making a dent!' he said. What was that thing made of?

His console beeped. Poe checked his scanner to find hundreds of seekers fired from hidden batteries. He'd encountered a few of these drone missiles during battles but never hundreds of them. Trying to shake them off would be near impossible.

'We got a lot of company!' Poe told his squadron mates. He managed to roll his starfighter to avoid getting hit from behind while shooting down seekers streaking at his X-wing's nose.

As skilled as they were, most of his squadron mates didn't have Poe's microsecond reflexes and intuition. They could elude five seekers in a series of incredible manoeuvres but then find themselves on a collision course with a sixth. And it took only one seeker to blow apart an X-wing.

The result was that Poe's two squadrons were decimated.

But he refused to give up hope. Not when Finn was down there. The renegade stormtrooper had rescued Poe from a fate worse than death on the Star Destroyer. Finn and his band would find some way to make this right.

Finn found an emergency hatch that led outside Starkiller Base. Though midday, the sunlight was diminishing rapidly, indicating that the Starkiller weapon was pulling in dark energy. Up in those gloomy skies, TIEs and seeker drones harried a much smaller group of X-wing fighters than had been originally dispatched. One of the X-wings – black with orange racing stripes – looped around a TIE. Finn exhaled in relief. Poe was still alive. But for how much longer, against such overwhelming numbers? Finn had to do something.

Han must've been thinking the same. 'Chewie here has a bag full of explosives that we didn't use inside. Be a shame to make him haul them all the way back to the *Falcon*. What's the best place we can use them?'

Since his friends in the skies were too busy dodging the enemy to make a bombing run, Finn realised there was only one place to go. 'The oscillator's the only sensible target. But there's no way to get inside.'

'There is a way,' Rey said.

They all looked at her. Chewbacca posed a question.

'I've seen inside these walls. The design mechanics are the same as the Star Destroyers I spent years salvaging. Get me to a junction station, I can get us into the oscillator.'

'If you can do that, we'll be ready,' Han said.

They hashed out a plan. Han and Chewie would head to the containment facility with the dentons. Meanwhile, Finn and Rey would find a craft to travel to a junction station where Rey would hot-wire the station to open the containment complex's doors. Once inside the facility, Han and Chewbacca would plant the explosives. Then Finn and Rey would swoop in to pick them up, and all four would head back to the *Falcon*.

Finn and Rey found their means of transportation at a nearby maintenance lot. Sneaking past the stormtrooper guard, the two climbed into an open-air snow speeder. The trooper spotted them as Rey started the engines, but by the time he fired his rifle, Rey had already flown away.

Laser fire from the starfighter battle struck the snow speeder's side. Rey fought to keep the vehicle aloft while Finn switched positions to target another snow speeder that was now chasing them.

Finn fired away, but his initial volleys missed. The pursuing pilot was a good one. But Finn had also become a pretty good gunner in recent days. His next round did not miss. 'Got him!'

Rey parked the speeder near the junction station and jumped out. She pried open a maintenance panel and began disconnecting wires.

On the horizon, Finn saw the rippling currents of dark energy being pulled into the containment facility. He had seen the same aerial pattern during tests of the Starkiller weapon. It was a sign that the weapon was on the verge of being completely charged.

Rey yanked out a clutch of flow fibres.

Finn couldn't see the end result of pulling those wires. He could only hope it opened the complex's doors.

Han and Chewie lurked near a service entrance to the containment facility. Three stormtroopers stood guard. When the service door suddenly opened behind the troopers, they turned in surprise. Chewbacca fired his bowcaster. One trooper fell, but the others whirled and fired. Their aim was off. Han's was not. He blasted both of them before they could fire another shot.

A fourth trooper on the other side of the door immediately withdrew. Han heard him call for help. But by the time any reinforcements could arrive, he and Chewie would have planted the explosives and started on their way back to the *Falcon* with the kids. Then back to D'Qar. Back to Leia.

They entered the facility. Machines buzzed and screens flashed, showing that the collected dark energy measured near peak levels. Destroying those devices wouldn't damage the weapon. Han considered the tall stone pillars connected at various levels by walkways. They appeared to support the entire structure. Perhaps if he and Chewie could topple them, they could collapse the roof. That would give Poe and his pilots an unobstructed shot at the weapon below.

Han grabbed some dentons from Chewbacca's sack. 'Let's plant 'em at every other support column we find.'

Chewbacca barked down that idea. Han rechecked the dentons. 'You're right. We don't have enough munitions to bring down more than one.' He pointed at the closest pillar. 'We'll put everything we've got into that one column. You take the top, I'll go below. We'll meet back here.'

They split, but Han hadn't taken more than a few steps before he glanced over his shoulder at his partner. Chewie did the same. They held that look, then parted to finish the job.

Han stuck the explosive charges around the base of the pillar and programmed each to detonate by remote activation. About to plant his final charge, he heard a clank. Han ducked behind a support beam and waited before he chanced a look.

His son peered down from a catwalk.

Whether he'd seen Han or not, Han couldn't tell. His son's eyes were hidden under that hideous metal mask. The mask that was the face of Kylo Ren.

Cape billowing behind him, his son descended to check the ground floor. Han stepped back into a dark alcove. He stood still when his son passed his hiding place. His own flesh and blood was so close, closer than he'd been in years. Han couldn't help reaching out to him. The young man was his son, after all.

'Ben,' he said.

His son turned at the name Han and Leia had given him. 'Han Solo,' he said to his father. 'I've been waiting for this day a long time.'

Han stepped out of the alcove. 'Take off that mask. You don't need it. Not here. Not with me.'

The mask's molded expression mocked Han. 'What do you think you'll see if I take it off?'

'The face of my son,' Han said.

'Your son is gone. He was weak and foolish, like his father. So I destroyed him.' Black-gloved hands rose to pull off the mask.

Ben had the wavy dark hair that Han remembered, now shoulder length. His mother's cheeks, Han's chin. Yet everything about him was narrow and stark, as if he had starved himself of nourishment. And his eyes were not the brown eyes Han remembered. They were dim and dark and terribly sad.

'That's what Snoke wants you to believe,' Han answered. 'It's not true. My son is still alive. I'm looking at him right now.'

Ben sneered. 'No. The Supreme Leader is wise. He knows you for what you really are, Han Solo.'

A stormtrooper squad clattered to a halt behind Ben. Han knew Chewbacca would be aiming the bowcaster from above. He also knew that Chewie wouldn't shoot unless Han gave the signal.

Han stepped closer to his son. 'Snoke's using you for your power, manipulating your abilities. When he's gotten everything he wants out of you, he'll crush you. Toss you aside. You know it's true.'

Ben shook his head. 'It's too late.'

'No, it's not. It's never too late for the truth. Leave here with me. Come home. Your mother misses you.'

Ben's narrow eyes narrowed further. Did Han spy a glimmer of tears? Perhaps Leia was right. Perhaps he could save Ben as Luke had saved his father.

'I'm being torn apart,' Ben said, his voice trembling. 'I want . . . I want to be free of this pain.'

Han halted on the walkway. His son started towards him. 'I know what I have to do, but I don't know if I have the strength to do it. Will you help me?'

Han answered as any father would. 'Yes. Anything.'

Ben unbelted his lightsaber hilt and held it out. Han looked at the hilt and then at his son. Finally, he reached for it.

'Thank you,' Ben said. He ignited the lightsaber.

At first, Han didn't feel anything except a piercing heat in his chest. Then his lungs didn't work. His heart stopped beating. His legs wobbled. He lost his feet. The fiery blade sank deeper. And he knew that this time, this impossible situation was one Chewie couldn't save him from.

In the last few seconds of his life, he thought of the *Falcon* and his furry first mate and his beautiful princess, but he saw only his son. The darkness in his eyes. And the sadness.

Han forgave his son for what he had done. He prayed someday his son would forgive him in turn.

CHAPTER
20

ON a catwalk in the facility, Finn gasped. Below, one of the galaxy's last legends crumpled. He had been a famous hero of the Rebellion. Record holder of the Kessel Run. Captain of the renowned *Millennium Falcon*.

Kylo Ren withdrew the lightsaber from his corpse. Han Solo was dead.

'No,' was all Rey could say, 'no, no, no . . .'

Finn put his arm around her. The two had just entered the facility to tell Han they had a speeder and were ready to go. Not to watch him die. Not to hear a bellowing howl so deep and deafening that if they had been any closer, their ear drums might have shattered.

From a lower catwalk, Chewbacca roared and fired his bowcaster.

The quarrel struck Kylo Ren square in the side. He fell back onto the walkway.

The squad of stormtroopers behind Ren fired up at the Wookiee. Chewbacca downed a couple of them, then retreated into a corridor. Before he disappeared, Finn saw him tap an activation remote.

The charges around the column blinked, then one after another detonated. Blasted apart, the stone column toppled like a giant tree. Losing the structural support to hold up the dense bomb-proof cement, the roof cracked and rained down rubble.

Kylo Ren crawled back onto his feet. He looked up and saw Finn and Rey. Some of the squad followed Ren's gaze and opened fire on them.

Rey shot back. Finn did not. He needed both hands to pull her away before the rubble buried them.

Chewbacca thundered down the corridor, bellowing in rage. He had surrendered all caution to berserker fury. He wanted any First Order troopers who dared to stop him to know that he would be their death.

For those few who tried, he was.

One trooper received a bowcaster quarrel in the chest. Another pair he hurled down intersecting corridors to be toasted by their comrades' blaster fire. The sentry at the door couldn't get out of the complex in time.

For him, Chewbacca extended his claws.

The Wookiee honour code forbade their use for anything other than climbing. But there was no honour among these First Order vermin. Kylo Ren had broken all the rules when he committed patricide, murdering the man who was not only his father but Chewbacca's closest and dearest friend – Han Solo.

Solo. For some his friend's surname seemed to fit his personality. But not for Chewbacca. Despite sometimes making it look like he was a lone operator, Han never did anything by himself. Chewbacca wouldn't let him. The two had sacrificed everything to help each other. Their ties were as tight as family.

Han *was* Chewbacca's family.

Chewbacca howled, clawing through the gaps in the sentry's armour until the soldier writhed no more.

Dropping the trooper, Chewbacca punched the access panel. The blast door opened.

Outside, the frozen landscape awaited him. A gust of wind ruffled his pelt, an icy reminder of what he had lost and where he was going.

Chewbacca almost turned around. He almost rushed right back into the complex. It would be suicide. But it might give him another chance at that traitor, that abomination of a son. He doubted that a single quarrel had been enough to kill Kylo Ren.

But Chewbacca had witnessed death many times, along with the barrenness of revenge. Killing Kylo Ren would not give him any satisfaction, because it would not save Han.

The kids. Save the kids.

The thought came to him in Han's gruff voice. He

hesitated in the doorway. He knew it wasn't Han speaking from the grave. Chewbacca wasn't the superstitious type. It was just something his partner would've said, in his irritable manner, griping that he'd once again have to risk his hide for someone else.

That was Han. Always grumbling. Always doing the right thing.

Chewbacca ran out into the snow, towards a nearby snow speeder. He squeezed himself into the speeder, engaged the repulsors, and zoomed towards the *Falcon*.

The snow speeder's scanners alerted him in advance that six stormtroopers guarded the Corellian freighter. Chewbacca readied the vehicle's cannons. He downed three troopers before the guards realised he wasn't a First Order pilot. The rest returned fire, missing when Chewbacca cut the engines and jumped out of the speeder. Charging forward, he triggered his bowcaster and knocked two troopers off the boarding ramp.

The last stormtrooper darted into the *Falcon*. Before the trooper could touch the panel to close the hatch, Chewbacca reached out with a long arm and grabbed the underside of his helmet. Yanked backward, the trooper landed atop his comrades in the snow.

Chewbacca went straight into the cockpit. He dropped into Han's seat and started the launch sequence. His paws could move over the controls faster than even

Han's. He'd never told Han that, out of respect for the smuggler's fragile ego.

It was an argument he wished they could still have.

Finn tugged Rey into the forest. When they thought they had put a good distance between themselves and their enemies, they slowed to catch their breaths.

'Stop,' someone commanded.

The distance was not enough. Somehow Kylo Ren had found them. The young man, who without his mask looked barely older than Finn, took out his lightsaber and marched towards them. Chewbacca's quarrel had burned a hole through his robes and shattered the armour around his torso. From the looks of it, he was wounded badly.

Rey drew her blaster. Ren lifted his arm and stretched out his hand towards Rey. To Finn's astonishment, Rey's trigger finger seemed to freeze and the blaster flew out of her hand.

Ren made another quick motion with his arm and Rey herself was hurled into a tree like a limp puppet. 'Rey!' Finn shouted. 'Rey!'

She couldn't answer, in a daze of pain.

Ren activated his blade. It flickered like a sword of pure fire and cast a hot red glow on the snow. Out of reach of Rey's blaster, Finn drew the only weapon he had. The lightsaber of Luke Skywalker.

Ren hesitated, seeing the blue blade spring to life. 'That weapon,' he said, 'is mine.'

Finn motioned with his lightsaber. 'Come and get it.'

'I'm going to kill you for it,' Ren said, and charged.

Finn blocked and parried the first flurry of Ren's attacks. Ground snow melted as the tips of their blades swooshed low. Finn could not find an opening in Ren's defences, despite the man's injury. Ren drove Finn back, seeming to draw strength from Finn's frustration.

Training had taught Finn to bait an opponent into thinking he had the advantage. Finn parried weakly, then disengaged and stabbed. His blade tip sheared Ren's arm. It didn't do much more than sizzle his opponent's skin. But Ren backpedalled, reassessing Finn.

Holding the blue blade in front of him, Finn stared at Kylo Ren, ready for anything.

But he was not ready for the fury of the attack Ren launched at him. It was as if the previous back and forth had been child's play. Ren's swings flew at Finn fast and strong, pushing him back.

Ren's blade gashed open Finn's chest. Finn fell back, and the momentum of his last swing threw the lightsaber of Luke Skywalker well away from him. He saw the blue blade dissolve back into the hilt, and then his universe turned dark.

———

Kylo Ren didn't give FN-2187 another glance after delivering his final stroke. He retracted his blade, turned and reached out a hand for Finn's lightsaber.

The hilt wobbled in the snow. Pulling it through the Force proved more strenuous than it should. The pain of Ren's wound clouded his concentration.

Ren tugged harder. The hilt sprang free of the snow – and shot past Ren into Rey's hand.

She stood by the tree he had hurled her into, looking wide-eyed at the weapon as if she couldn't believe she held it. 'It is you,' Ren said.

Her surprise shifted to anger. Ren could feel it, like waves of heat radiating off of her. She wanted to strike back at him for what he had done to her friends. He stood there, daring her to do so with his stare.

The girl switched on the lightsaber and rushed him.

Ren ignited his own blade and parried her attack. He countered; she blocked, then went in for another attack. While her sword strokes were unpolished, it was clear she knew how to fight with hand-to-hand weapons. Her blade smashed against his, over and over, never buckling, at times forcing him back.

She was also angry. She drew her power from the same well as Ren – her rage. And that would be the weakness he would use to defeat her. Kylo Ren had more rage than she would ever know.

He lashed out with his lightsaber, chopping and

slicing. She deflected him but could not sustain her defense without stepping back. And back. And back.

Without warning or sign, the roof of the containment facility exploded.

No X-wing bomb had hit it. Detonations inside the complex had triggered the collapse. How Finn and his band had managed it, Poe didn't know; he just thanked the stars they had.

Poe commed the few squad mates he had left. 'All units, target structural integrity has been breached. I repeat – target integrity has been breached! There's an opening. Now's our chance. Hit it hard and don't miss!'

The X-wings stopped their evasive manoeuvres and jetted after him towards the containment facility. One by one, they dropped their bombs. Explosions rocked the facility. Finally, the structure could take no more. In a thunderous boom that shook the mountains, the complex caved in on itself. Fire surged around it into the skies. The oscillator in the planetary core began to implode.

The world shook.

The detonations had reached the planetary core, inducing tectonic shifts in the continents and immediate changes on the surface. Trees swayed – and bent. An entire swath of forest was laid low. A giant fissure opened in the ground and swallowed most of it. Dust billowed out. Within seconds, Rey was standing at the edge of a cliff. She had no more ground to lose.

Ren pointed his lightsaber at her. 'I could kill you, right now. But there is another way.'

Rey snarled at him. 'You're a monster.'

'No. You need a teacher,' he said. 'I can show you the ways of the Force!'

'"The Force"?' she repeated, sounding confused and exasperated all at once. She closed her eyes for a moment, then lunged at Ren again, more furious than before. And for once, Kylo Ren dueled an opponent who had more anger than he. Or maybe what fueled her wasn't anger. Maybe it was an emotion he didn't recognise anymore. Whatever it was, it took him down.

Staggering back to his feet, his parry could not match the strength of her swing. It cast his lightsaber out of his grasp.

Ren extended a hand, calling on the Force to ward off her attacks. At first it worked, as she slashed into the iron shield of his will, but then her blade cut across his face. It burned.

He looked up at the girl whose lightsaber hovered over his chest. He shivered under the coldness of her stare. He who had been so eager to kill was not eager to die. Kylo Ren was afraid.

The girl withdrew from him.

Ren watched her walk back to the prone form of FN-2187. She had the chance to kill him, yet did not. Did the girl think she was actually stronger than him? Or worse, did she *pity* him?

The ground heaved and fractured between Ren and the two youths. She did not look back at Ren, but he sneered at her. While the planet erupted around her, the girl knelt to cradle the body of her friend. She was such a fool. She would die there.

Kylo Ren would not. A shuttle landed nearby. General Hux and a group of stormtroopers leapt out. Hux must have traced Ren's location through the transmitter on Ren's belt.

The stormtroopers lifted Ren and transferred him into the shuttle. A smug General Hux walked beside them. Ren did not show the general any appreciation for the rescue. That Hux had bothered to retrieve him only meant that the Supreme Leader had commanded it.

Kylo Ren would save all his gratitude for his master.

The Starkiller weapon could kill no more. The planet itself was about to blow.

Poe's comm nearly shorted out from BB-8's triumphant trills and the shrieks of joy from his squad mates. Poe added some of his own.

He was about to instruct BB-8 to search for any humans around the facility when his scanner readout showed a Corellian freighter that identified itself as the *Millennium Falcon* lifting off from the surface. A Wookiee roar over the comm confirmed that the ground team had made its escape.

Pulling back on his yoke, Poe led the X-wings up through the gloom and far, far away to the stars.

CHAPTER
21

TRIUMPHANT cheers echoed far and wide across the base on D'Qar. The battle was over. Starkiller Base was destroyed. The Resistance had won.

General Leia Organa retired to her quarters and wept.

Moments before the command centre holoscreens had relayed the detonations, she had felt the sharpest and deepest of pains. As if her heart had ruptured.

Her husband. Han. He was gone.

Those who knew Leia considered her to be someone who had suffered much yet had always emerged from that suffering stronger and wiser. But immersed in her present grief, Leia found no strength. She found no wisdom. She found only anguish and emptiness. She'd failed to prevent her son from succumbing to the darkness of Darth Vader. Now her husband was dead. Her brother lost.

Would it ever end?

She doubted it would. But if she surrendered, who else would disappear? How many more homes and husbands and sons and brothers would vanish like hers?

Leia did not view herself as strong or wise. She was, if anything, persistent.

Steeled by that persistence, she strode out of her quarters and onto the tarmac to greet those who had returned from enemy territory.

C-3PO and BB-8 joined Leia as the *Millennium Falcon* landed. A crowd formed behind her. The freighter's hatch opened, but all cheering was respectfully muted when Chewbacca ran down the ramp carrying a severely wounded Finn. A medical team assisted him immediately.

The applause came back loud and triumphant for the girl who emerged next. She descended the ramp and walked over to Leia.

Leia held Rey's face in her hands, then embraced her, sharing the girl's tears.

Poe went to the situation room, taking BB-8 with him. A host of senior commanders and officers had assembled there, along with the girl from Jakku, General Organa, and her protocol droid. They had gathered to discuss the still unknown whereabouts of Luke Skywalker.

Poe started the conversation. 'Kylo Ren said to me that the segment held by Beebee-Ate is the last piece of the map that shows the way to Skywalker's location. So where's the rest of it?'

The girl chimed in. 'The First Order has it. They extracted it from the Imperial archives.'

Poe blinked in surprise. 'The Empire?'

'It makes sense,' said Admiral Statura. 'The Empire would've been looking for the first Jedi temples. In destroying all the Jedi sanctuaries, they would have acquired a great deal of information.'

Poe had nothing to say to that. His eye strayed from Statura to a light that had switched on in the back of the room. Seemingly forgotten among a pile of discarded equipment was an old R2-class astromech droid.

'We're still at war with the First Order – a war that won't end until they or the Resistance is destroyed,' General Organa said. 'The next time without Luke, we won't stand a chance.'

The old R2 unit trundled forward into the gathering. It issued forth a stream of beeps that were every bit as loud as anything BB-8 produced.

'Artoo, what is it?' an oddly excited C-3PO asked. 'I haven't seen you this functional since . . . slow down! You're giving me data overload!'

The R2 unit did not slow down, whistling and tootling as if his electronic existence depended on it. 'What's he saying?' General Organa asked.

C-3PO translated. 'He says if the information you are

seeking was in the Imperial archives, he may have it in his memory. He's scanning through the records now.'

The general gaped at the astromech droid. 'Artoo has the rest of the map?'

'He's certainly implying the possibility,' C-3PO said, his voice high-pitched. 'I've never heard him beep with this much energy before!'

R2-D2 hooted, then projected a hologram from his lens. Before them all hovered an enormous galactic map, far larger and more detailed than the one obtained from Lor San Tekka. Yet as before, an area of the map was blank, missing information.

BB-8 beeped and nudged Poe. 'Yeah, buddy, hold on,' Poe said. 'I have it.'

Poe took out the peculiar object Lor San Tekka had given him and the Resistance had returned to him. He inserted it into BB-8's data port. The droid sat still for a moment, reading its contents. Then BB-8 projected a star chart of his own. Once its proportions were adjusted, the smaller map filled in the gap in the bigger map.

C-3PO cheered. 'Oh, my stars – that's it! Artoo! Artoo, you've done it!'

A less excited but more touching response came from General Organa. 'Luke . . .'

The name electrified the room. Officers who had never shown emotion embraced each other. Poe mused that yet again, all the tiny victories had contributed to something greater.

The girl from Jakku stood next to him. Unsure of whether to embrace someone he barely knew, he introduced himself. 'Uh, hi, I'm Poe.'

'So you're Poe,' she said. 'Poe Dameron. The X-wing pilot. I'm Rey.'

'I know,' Poe said. 'Nice to meet you.'

They traded smiles. Poe had a feeling their paths would soon cross again.

Rey wanted to say goodbye to Finn before she left on her mission, even though she knew he wouldn't hear her. He lay in a coma in the base's medical centre, still on life support.

Doctor Kalonia, the same physician who had treated Chewbacca, assured Rey her friend was going to be fine. But that had been a few days before, and Finn's condition remained the same.

Rey sat with Finn for what must've been hours. When it was time to leave, she bent over his recovery pod and kissed him. 'We'll see each other again. I believe that. Thank you, my friend.'

Rey headed to the launch area with R2-D2. Leia waited near the boarding ramp. She adjusted the fit of the new flight jacket Rey wore. 'I'm proud of what you're about to do.'

Rey looked into Leia's eyes and saw more than pride. 'But you're also afraid. In sending me away, you're . . . reminded.'

Leia let go of the girl's jacket. 'You won't share the fate of our son.'

Rey glanced at the *Falcon*. Chewbacca had almost completed his exterior flight check. 'I know what we're doing is right,' Rey said. 'This is how it has to be. This is how it *should* be.'

'I know it, too,' Leia said. 'May the Force be with you.' She moved back and smiled as Rey boarded.

Rey took the pilot's seat, which was where Chewbacca had asked her to sit. Despite the old cushioning, she felt comfortable in it.

Chewbacca scruffed up her hair and sat in the copilot's chair. R2-D2 rolled in behind them and chirped.

Rey refamiliarised herself with the controls, gauges and readouts. She didn't have to worry about the compressor or priming the fuel line. Chewbacca had yanked out everything Unkar Plutt had installed.

She engaged the repulsors, lifting the freighter from the tarmac. When the engines were ready, she took a breath and launched the *Millennium Falcon* towards a world that had been erased from the star charts - until now.

EPILOGUE

ONCE there was a mystical order of Jedi Knights who served as the guardians of peace and justice in the galaxy. Many were the heroes in their ranks. Heroes that went by the names of Obi-Wan Kenobi, Yoda and Anakin Skywalker. But like the Republic they defended, the Jedi were betrayed from within. Their order was extinguished, and despite great effort to rekindle it decades later, the new flame would not hold. The Jedi remained all but extinct.

Once there was a girl who called herself Rey. She had lived alone for years, until she recognised the value of family and friends. With two of these friends, she piloted a starship to a remote world. She landed on an island surrounded by a blue-green sea. Stone stairs carved into the island's mountain led her to a clearing. Here waited the hermit she had come to find.

Once there was a man who was born with the name Luke Skywalker. It was not a name he had been called in a long, long time. He lived alone, inhabiting this peaceful island on this lost planet. He allowed the girl to stare at him before he removed his hood. His robes were simple, his hair was white. A beard separated him from his youth, just as the remoteness of this planet separated him from his past. But now he had been found.

Once there was a lightsaber that had passed from one hand to another. Its blade was bright, its colour blue. The girl who possessed it now held it out to the man who had possessed it long before. He looked at her and then at the hilt in her hand – as if it were a memory he had tried to forget.

Once there was great knowledge of the Force, an energy field created by all living things that bound the galaxy together. The Force was what gave the Jedi their power. It had allowed them to accomplish great physical and mental feats and to turn the ordinary into the extraordinary. Yet when the Jedi were hunted down and destroyed, knowledge of the Force seemed to die with them. For many years afterward, individuals sensitive to the Force possessed neither the instruction nor the insight to properly call on it. Its true power remained dormant in their lives, a potential never tapped. Eventually, scarce evidence of its presence led few to believe that the Force had ever existed at all.

Yet within the girl and the man and the lightsaber held between, the Force stirred anew.

ABOUT THE AUTHOR

MICHAEL KOGGE'S other recent work includes *Empire of the Wolf*, an epic graphic novel featuring werewolves in ancient Rome, and the *Star Wars Rebels* series of books. He resides online at www.MichaelKogge. com, while his real home is in Los Angeles.